TO BE CONTINUED: TAKE TWO

EDITED BY

MICHELE KARLSBERG &
KAREN X. TULCHINSKY

Firebrand
Books

Ithaca, New York

Book design by Nightwood and Sunset Design
Cover design by Nightwood

Printed in Canada

10 9 8 7 6 5 4 3 2 1

Library of Congress Cataloging-in-Publication Data

To be continued, take two / edited by Michele Karlsberg and Karen X. Tulchinsky.
     p.   cm.
    Contents: Three weddings / Lucy Jane Bledsoe — Road maps / Nisa Donnelly — Joe Louis was a heck of a fighter / Jewelle Gomez — Apostate princess / Judith Katz — Fear / Randye Lordon — Pearl fishers / Linda Nelson — Shadow line / Elisabeth Nonas — Dragon's daughter / Cecilia Tan — Huevos rancheros / Carla Trujillo — Skinner and Choy / Kitty Tsui — To the flames / Jess Wells.
    ISBN 1-56341-111-3 (cloth : alk. paper). — ISBN 1-56341-110-5 (pbk. : alk. paper)
    1. Lesbians—Social life and customs—Fiction. 2. Lesbians' writings, American. 3. Short stories, American—Women authors. I. Karlsberg, Michele. II. Tulchinsky, Karen X.
PS648.L47T63   1999
813'.01089206643—dc21   99-14947
                                      CIP

ACKNOWLEDGMENTS

My co-editor, Karen X. Tulchinsky: I am honored to work with a wonderful editor.

Nancy K. Bereano: Proud that you are my publisher, even prouder to call you my friend.

The writers included in this collection: Assembling writers of your literary excellence is a treasured gift.

The late Stan Leventhal: Continuing in your footsteps.

Richard Labonte: You mean the world to me.

Allison and Heather Karlsberg, Mom, Grandma, and Aunt Jay: Thank you for your support and love.

The Girls Club: Your strengths and humor support me through all.

Latifah A. Rabb, Robert Kelly, Steven Cotugno, Lisa Pilkington, Lorraine Donald, Hazel Brown, Fred Brown, John Michael, Kerri O'Neill, Paul Lannigan, Francisca Reyes, Reggie Covington, Pedro Perez, Asa Berggren, The Grecos, Diane Sabin, M. Weston, Karen Lynch, Roz Parr, Sandy Brown, Maria Gattuso, Gerry Piserchia, and

Valerie Sagaria: We hustle through life together and hasn't it been fun?

Victoria Werner: Looking forward to a lifetime of love and friendship.

Earnestine Lannigan: Soaring into the future together, you know the sentiments.

Michele Karlsberg

Many thanks to:

Nancy K. Bereano for her vision and publishing expertise, and the women of Firebrand for their hard work and dedication in bringing this and other fine books to publication.

Michele Karlsberg, my co-editor, for her enthusiasm, hard work, and promotional expertise. It's always a pleasure to work with her, a dedicated publicist, editor, and curator of queer and feminist literature.

Richard Banner, Margaret Matsuyama, Trish Burleigh, Frances Wasserlein, Victoria Chan, and Victor Aker for computer advice and assistance, and for bailing me out of hard drive, megabyte, formatting, and other high tech emergencies.

My "other" co-editor, James C. Johnstone, for continual support, encouragement, friendship, secretarial assistance, and fabulous dinners.

Dianne Whelan for my author photo, friendship, and endless professional and philosophical conversations.

Other friends and colleagues: Lee McArthur, Maike Engelbrecht, Sandra Fellner, Brian Lam.

The wonderful, talented authors whose stories appear in *To Be Continued: Take Two*. It's been an honor to work with all of you.

Terrie Hamazaki, my fiancée, who continues to shower me with love, encouragement, support (and a few of my other favorite things), and Charlie Tulchinsky-Hamazaki, for knowing just the right moment to sit on my keyboard, signaling a much required break.

Karen X. Tulchinsky

A NOTE FROM THE EDITORS

Continuing stories have a long tradition.

In Victorian England, many fiction writers first published their novels as serializations in local newspapers. Charles Dickens' *Great Expectations* was among the novels first appearing one chapter at a time.

The early U.S. film industry followed this literary example. During the 1930s and '40s, you could go to the "picture show" for a nickel and, after the opening newsreel, catch up on the next episode of *Flash Gordon*, or your favorite western or melodrama. They were presented as half-hour serials, to be continued the following week. In addition, on radio programs of the era, serials were practically a staple item.

Television, of course, employs this very model on a regular basis—with each weekly episode drawing on the last. While soap operas stick the closest to the ongoing serial model, even sit-coms and hour-long dramas complete each week in themselves build on the situations and characters from past programs. A new viewer to a show can enjoy that single episode, yet long-term viewers' enjoyment is enhanced by their awareness of the subtle nuances of character and plot development which unfold over time.

Since the famous *Dallas* pre-summer season finale which left viewers wondering who *did* shoot JR?, other shows have used a cliffhanger on the last episode, picking up the story line when the season begins again in the fall.

To Be Continued... and *To Be Continued: Take Two* follow in this long-established tradition. For the first book, we invited eleven talented, seasoned lesbian authors to write a short story which was complete in itself, but also ended on an unresolved climactic moment. The stories we received were wonderfully diverse in style and content, and each lived up to our original expectations of excellence.

Like the first volume, the stories in the companion *To Be Continued: Take Two* stand on their own. We hope you choose to read both books because we think you'll enjoy them, but regardless of your reading choices, we are pleased to report that just like *To Be Continued...*, the pieces in this volume are humorous, literate, and passionate. You will find fantasy, romance, herstory, intrigue, and suspense written by some of the best creators of contemporary lesbian fiction.

Michele Karlsberg and Karen X. Tulchinsky

for Aunt Jay and Earnie
MK

for Cookie
KXT

CONTENTS

THREE WEDDINGS

LUCY Jane BLEDSOE

withered under Marcia's glare, regretting what I had just done to my oldest friend. What was wrong with me? Sure I hated her partner, Carrie, but I loved Marcia. Not only had I wandered off and missed her wedding, I had taken her mother with me.

Mrs. Michaelson and I sat on the edge of the red clay cliff over which we had just climbed after a little expedition down to the beach. The Pacific Ocean stretched out before us, cool and edgy under pillows of fog that still, though it was well into afternoon, hadn't burned off. However, Mrs. Michaelson and I weren't gazing at the ocean and clouds. We were, instead, clutching our heaping plates of beans and looking over our shoulders at glaring Marcia, guilty as dogs with the holiday turkey in our jaws.

I had never seen Marcia's face so red nor her lips so white. Her eyes had a wide-open shocked look, as if she had just suffered a trauma to the head. She had every right to be furious with me, but I was a little taken aback by the degree of devastation her mother and I had caused by missing the exchange of vows. I would have thought she would let us have it later, not right here and now at her wedding.

Of course Marcia would believe I had missed the ceremony on purpose. She knew I disliked her girlfriend. Thin and pale, Carrie Byrd taught literature at a local, and not particularly prestigious, college. Yet you would think she was the fucking Poet Laureate for how she talked about books. I mean, why couldn't she just say, "Yeah, that dyke character was hot." But no. Instead it would be, "Considering the contextual gender delineations, which is to say the blending of masculine and feminine components in the body per se, the protagonist compels the reader to feel an exertion on her constructs of desire." When she talked like that, the blue vein at her temple pulsed with excitement.

"Whatever gets you hot, babe," I would tell her, and then receive a fierce *behave* look from Marcia, the kind I've been getting for thirty years. I couldn't imagine what kind of sex they had. I mean, get this: Carrie called herself an "academic butch." I kid you not. I have more butch in my little finger than she has in her entire body. She loved to say that, though, *academic butch*, and then laugh. I never laughed. It wasn't funny.

"You hate everyone I've ever been with," Marcia recently accused me.

"You do have bad taste when it comes to lovers."

"Bonnie!"

"It's just that everything Carrie does is for the promotion of Carrie. I'm afraid she'll chew you up and spit you out."

"I'm not going to have that argument again. I want you at the ceremony, but you don't *have* to come."

Of course I came. And blew it big time.

"I'm sorry, Marcia." I set down my plate of high-fiber food and scrambled to my feet, then paused, figuring that Mrs. Michaelson would also offer an apology and get up, but she remained quiet and seated on the muddy cliff, gazing out at the sea. So I repeated myself. "I'm really, really sorry, Marcia. The ocean looked so beautiful and we thought we'd just go for a little walk and I didn't think the ceremony would begin for another—"

"It's not that!" Marcia cried.

I was stunned. She wasn't angry we had missed her wedding? Then what?

Uh-oh. I thought the answer hovered a few feet beyond Marcia's right shoulder—Viola Mendoza, her best friend from the literary magazine collective. Marcia had insisted that I not flirt with Viola, and had specifically asked me to refrain from doing so at her wedding. To which I had responded, "Next you'll tell me I can't eat anything at your wedding, either. What is this?"

"It makes me jealous. I don't want to have to feel jealous at my own wedding."

"Marcia, love. Let's be real. We were together when we were eighteen. We're dangerously close to fifty now."

"I know," she pouted and gave me that look. The one that still, thirty years later, made me want something powerful from her. "Please, Bonnie," was her sincere, sweet way of telling me to behave. She kissed my ear and linked her pinkie with mine. It was a game we played, pretending we were still eighteen, as if we still rocked each other's worlds. The thing is, Marcia *had* rocked my world. She brought me out. We've remained friends all these years, in spite of our vast differences. And, of course, I'll never forget that it was her father who got me into law school and who kept me there. To Marcia's credit, she never refers to that, might even have forgotten it. But I'll never forget it.

She said, "You know what I mean, Bon. We're like soul sisters."

"And you're marrying someone else. Shouldn't you be worried about who *she's* flirting with?"

I had put my foot in it. Her eyes shrouded over and she clamped her lips. She admitted, "I don't need it from both of you on my wedding day."

"Your second wedding day."

"Bonnie, please—"

"Act right."

"Exactly. But there's a better reason for why you shouldn't flirt with Viola."

"I bet you'll tell me what it is, too."

"She's married."

"Yeah, I know. That's what makes the flirting so exciting."

"No, that's what makes the flirting so safe. Why don't you try flirting with someone who is available for once."

"So when did you get your psych degree?"

"It's been five years since you broke up with Rosie, and how many since you've had sex? With anyone?"

"Dangerous territory, babe."

"I'd say at least three years. The last I can remember is that bimbo you picked up at the magazine's fundraiser. Is there something you particularly enjoy about picking up girls under my nose?"

I smiled. "Yeah. I guess there is."

And now I had done it again. Flirted under her nose. At her own wedding. With her other best friend, the one with whom she forbid me to flirt. She should have known that her forbidding only threw gas on the fire, made it burn hotter. Anyway, I liked Viola Mendoza. She always wore that ponytail with lots of breakaway wisps, as if she didn't quite have time to do anything else with her hair. She had dynamite cheekbones and a chunky, athletic body.

Viola's girlfriend, Maxine, who stood by her side now, a few yards back from the cliff where I sat, was, like Carrie Byrd another faux butch. She was much younger than Viola. I'm sure she couldn't have been a day over thirty-five. Trim and fit, tanned year round, with short blonde, sculpted hair, she wore tiny gold jewelry—the little gold balls on her ears, the one gold chain around her neck with a tiny heart linked onto it, and the gold wedding band from her commitment ceremony with Viola. I never quite understood why they were together except that they seemed to share a love of the outdoors. Lots of hiking, cycling, and sea kayaking. Maxine's truck always looked like a fucking REI outlet, loaded to the gills with equipment. Now, sitting on this cliff, looking up at Marcia and beyond her to Viola and Maxine, I felt as if I were in a lesbian diorama, everyone frozen in their positions, everyone looking extremely pained. The educational caption would read: *Can you figure out what's going on with these women?*

Really, I decided, Marcia should be ashamed of herself for sniveling like this on her wedding day over my flirting with her friend. "For Pete's sake, pull yourself together, Marcia. Where's Carrie?"

"That's what I'm trying to tell you! She's backing out."

I glanced over at the gravel parking lot, and sure enough, there was Carrie in her Honda Civic, backing out. A terrible silence, broken only by the crashing waves and the crunch of gravel under the tires of Carrie's car, took hold of the entire grassy wedding site. "Where is she going? What about the reception? Is she okay?"

"Bonnie," Mrs. Michaelson said, coming to her feet at last and speaking for her daughter because now Marcia was crying too hard to talk, "I think Marcia has just told us that Carrie backed out of everything."

"You mean we didn't miss the ceremony?" What a relief.

"I don't think there was a ceremony."

It took me a moment to realize that although I wasn't in trouble, Marcia was. Viola and Maxine approached cautiously. Viola put an arm around Marcia and dropped her forehead onto her friend's shoulder. Maxine hovered and popped her capable knuckles. As if we didn't have a big enough crowd, Jonathan, Marcia's ex-husband, and his wife Susan now joined us on the edge of the cliff. Jonathan patted Marcia's back. "I'm sorry, Marsh," he said. He had always called her that, as if she were a swamp. "God, I'm really sorry." Susan cocked her head and puckered her face in an expression of forced compassion. I thought divorce meant you got rid of the guy. Marcia not only spent time with her ex, she spent time with the new wife as well. Big heart, my Marcia.

Once again, it was left to me to clean up the mess. My initial impulse was to jump into my Cherokee and chase down Carrie. How dare she leave Marcia in the lurch! My second thought was good riddance. Carrie's desertion was actually very good news, but I had to get Marcia over the rough terrain. First things first. We had to clear out the wedding guests who hovered uncomfortably around the food table. Imagine their predicament. If one of the brides ditches the ceremony, what do you do? Get in your car and leave also? That seemed cold. Stand around gaping? Too rude. So they focused on the food, acted as if nothing had happened, waited for their cue. Thank God Mrs. Michaelson was ready to help me take charge.

"Jonathan, dear," she said, "why don't you go over and ask the guests to please just go home. And tell them to take as much of that rabbit food as they can carry."

"Mom! Don't be mean," Marcia whined.

"I'm not being mean. What can we do with all that food, dear?"

"You called it rabbit food."

"You don't eat that crap. Carrie did."

"Does."

"She's gone and we don't need it. Jonathan?"

Jonathan and Susan walked slowly toward the food table. Jonathan wasn't particularly assertive, and I could tell by his gait that this assignment unnerved him. How could a sensitive straight white man tell a bunch of dykes to clear away from a food table?

I followed, lending my voice of dyke authority to Jonathan's corralling efforts, and together we managed to clear out the wedding site in ten minutes. Then I sent Jonathan and Susan packing, though they tried to linger, asking about fifteen times what they could do to help. Finally I was forced to say, "The best thing you could do would be to leave." Jonathan looked hurt. He had accused me, more than once, of reverse discrimination. He was quite sure I hated men. Susan, on the other hand, bent over backwards to prove she wasn't afraid of me. Which of course meant that she was, at least a little bit. It's a cheap thrill, but I love the feeling anyway, straight women being a bit discombobulated by me.

Once I got them packed into their car, I returned to Marcia, Mrs. Michaelson, Maxine, and Viola. Marcia had begun to rant, which I took as a good sign, not just for this particular situation but for her overall development. I had never seen Marcia rant before, and it showed she was evolving. I urged them all toward my Cherokee and told them to get in, but Maxine insisted on following in her own truck. I couldn't help feeling good as I drove Marcia and her mother along the coast. I knew Marcia felt devastated, but I also knew it was the best thing that could have happened.

The late afternoon light was honeyed, sweet and sticky and golden. I drove slowly, as if there were someone injured in the car, and enjoyed the wide sweeps of coast that filled my windshield as I came around the bends on Route 1. Occasionally I glanced in my rearview mirror at Maxine behind the wheel of her truck and Viola in the passenger seat.

Earlier this week, Marcia bragged that Carrie had booked and prepaid for the honeymoon suite at the posh Seal Cove Inn, fifteen miles down the coast from the wedding knoll. I drove there now. The Seal Cove Inn was composed of ten guesthouses, all perched high on the cliffs above the opening of a harbor. The grounds were meticulously landscaped with blooming coastal plants, and soft green lawns separated each cottage from the next. After I checked in at the reception desk, pretending for the sake of simplicity to be Carrie Byrd, everyone got out of the trucks and we stood on the patio in front of the honeymoon suite, looking at the view. The orange sun hung over the horizon; a fishing boat chugged toward the harbor. Great foamy white splashes surged into the sky as the sea rolled toward the tiny harbor opening and crashed onto the cliffs.

"What are you doing, Bonnie?" Marcia asked. "Why are we here?"

"I have to say, I'm a little confused, too," Maxine piped up. "I guess I thought you were going back to the city. Or somewhere for tea. Isn't this…?"

"Let's just have a look inside," I said. "I thought we needed to go somewhere to chill a little. And this place was right here, all paid for, right?"

Maxine huffed the air out of her lungs and reared back her head. Like I was way out of line. But Mrs. Michaelson and Viola were right on my heels as I unlocked the suite and started to explore the austerely elegant rooms. First there was an entryway with an antique cabinet upon which sat a grotesquely big floral bouquet. A little card propped up next to the flowers read: *With love, from Jonathan and Susan.* Geez, would she never lose the guy? The main room held an enormous bed that was so high off the floor, I'd be afraid of falling out of it. Two plush armchairs faced the sliding glass door, looking out at the cliffs, splashing waves, and flaming horizon. On a table between the two armchairs was a scrumptious spread of appetizers, including smoked raw salmon, a couple of lobster tails, and fresh berries. Carrie must have forgotten to tell them that she ate only beans and carrots. A bottle of champagne chilled in a bucket of ice on the floor. Mrs. Michaelson caught my eye and winked. How long did we have to wait before digging in?

"What are we doing here?" Marcia cried, throwing herself face down on the bed.

"It's paid for, right?" I answered.

"Bonnie!"

"Look," I said. "This room is what, two or three hundred dollars?"

"Three-fifty," she muttered.

"Uh-huh. And it's all paid for?"

"Carrie paid for it in advance. It's her wedding present to me." Marcia paused and then added, "Even though she's broke." She cringed at her own absurd sentimentality.

"Okay," I said. "Look, the way I was raised, you don't flush three-fifty down the toilet. Carrie may have ditched the wedding, but we're not going to drain the baby out with the bath water."

"You're calling Carrie bath water!"

"For goodness sake, dear," Mrs. Michaelson said. "The woman just ran out on your wedding. That's a very clear message."

"You both always hated her."

"Maybe now you know why."

"Can we just leave?" Marcia said.

I argued, "I'm going to plunk down forty dollars for a room at a Motel 6 when this is paid for. I don't think so."

"Big deal. You make two hundred fifty thousand a year."

"Two hundred sixty-seven thousand."

"We can pay for another room."

As Marcia and I argued, Viola and Maxine stepped into the bathroom where I heard them arguing as well. When they reemerged, Maxine announced, "This is wrong. I don't feel comfortable with it."

"What's the problem, Max?" I loved calling her Max. It spoke to the butch in her that she worked so hard to repress.

"Isn't it obvious?"

"Clearly it isn't," Viola said. Marcia sat up and looked interested. While she had maintained that she wanted to leave, I think she knew that her mom, Viola, and I were definitely her advocates. Maxine said, "Carrie paid for this for her and Marcia. It's got to be painful for Marcia to be here. We should all go home."

"I guess it's Marcia's choice, isn't it?" Viola said. We all looked at Marcia.

"Your choice, babe," I said. "A three-hour drive on a bumpy, windy road—and you know how you get carsick—so you can return home to your cold, empty house by yourself...or, stay here and sleep on that plush bed, in a new setting that doesn't have painful memories attached to it, surrounded by the people who love you most in the world, so you can begin to recuperate and heal. What's your call?"

Out of the corner of my eye I saw Maxine give Viola a look that said something about my character. I should have just let it go, but it pissed me off. I turned and faced her. "Look, Max. Marcia and I have been friends since childhood. We came out together, okay? Don't think you know better about what she needs."

"Hey, chill," Maxine said, holding up her hands, palms out toward me. "Whoa."

"Don't 'whoa' me. I'm not a horse."

I loved that Viola laughed at that. I laughed too, then turned back to Marcia. She straightened her back and pouted. "It is paid for."

"I think it's disrespectful," Maxine dug in.

"To whom?" I said, purposely adding the *m* to ward off Maxine's making assumptions about me.

"If you want to leave, then leave," Viola said to her girlfriend. "I'll catch a ride with Bonnie."

"Fine. I can tell when I'm outnumbered. I'm not going to desert you, hon," she said to Viola.

"I'd be fine if you wanted to go home."

Maxine threw up her arms and forced a smile as if it had just been a slight difference of opinion. She draped an arm around Viola. "I'm with you, sweetie."

That little bogus display of loyalty and love affected Marcia, and she began crying again. I wondered if someday, *some day,* she would learn to differentiate between the real thing and bad copies. "I'll run her a tub," Viola said. While she and Maxine helped Marcia into the bathroom, playing with the gold fixtures to fill the small swimming pool with steaming hot water, Mrs. Michaelson and I settled into the two easy chairs in front of the setting-sun view. The horizon was a fiery orange fading to a golden yellow. The boisterous seas had calmed and now stretched glassily from harbor to horizon.

"There are only two lobster tails," Mrs. Michaelson pointed out.

I looked over my shoulder. I could hear little splashing sounds as Marcia stepped into the hot tub and the murmuring of Viola's voice. "They won't even remember they were here if we polish them off now," I suggested.

"Aren't you the only one who eats flesh anyway?" she asked.

"I believe I am."

I popped open the bottle of ice-cold champagne and filled the two flutes. We enjoyed the lobster tails immensely. I was licking each of my ten fingers, making sure to get every drop of lobster juice, when Viola and Maxine emerged from the bathroom. Not a minute too soon, I thought, though I supposed we'd have to share the champagne. But no, after pausing and looking at us for a moment, me with my index finger in my mouth, they proceeded outdoors to argue some more. Mrs. Michaelson and I had time for a nice long chat as we drank the champagne. When Marcia came out of the bathroom, wrapped in the thick terrycloth robe supplied by the inn, I felt quite relaxed. I called the reception desk and ordered two more bottles of champagne. Then, after propping Marcia up with pillows on the bed, I stepped out on the porch, where I found Viola bent at the waist, slapping the back of her hand into her other palm, making one of apparently several heated points.

"Ladies," I said, "I've just ordered a couple more bottles of champagne. Join us?"

"Perfect timing," Viola said, her eyes still scowling and fierce but her mouth loosening into a smile. "We were just arguing about sumptuousness."

"Do you think you could keep our issues private?" Maxine asked. She eyed me suspiciously, as if I reeked of champagne. Maxine always made me feel fat.

"I'd love some champagne," Viola said, and they both followed me inside.

"Damn," I said. "There are only these two flutes and a couple of bathroom drinking glasses. Max, you must have a thermal camping mug in your truck, no?"

"I don't need any champagne."

"Don't be silly!" I said simultaneously with Viola saying she'd go get something from the truck. "Now," I said, after the champagne had arrived and everyone had a drinking vessel, "will someone please tell me exactly what happened at the wedding?"

Clean and warm from her hot tub, wrapped in comforters and supported by pillows, Marcia drank her big glass of champagne right down. "Shit," she said. "My mom and my best friends. What more could I want?"

"That's the spirit," I encouraged. "What happened?"

Marcia began the story back a lot further than I had intended. We all heard about how Carrie Byrd seduced her three years ago, how from the very start she had campaigned for a wedding, how eventually she had accused Marcia of being afraid of commitment if she didn't agree to the ceremony. But when it came to telling what actually happened at the wedding, Marcia broke down crying and couldn't continue. So while glum Maxine took tiny, occasional sips of champagne from her insulated mug, Viola told Mrs. Michaelson and me the rest of the story. Marcia had said her vows. I could see it perfectly— that cute little shy smile, her eyes wide and absolutely trusting. How does a person get that way? Absolutely trusting. Then it was Carrie's turn to say the vows, the vows they had spent months writing together, rewriting, reading both ancient and New Age texts, looking for the perfect words of commitment. Carrie, and I can picture her too, with her hard eyes that dared anyone to challenge her integrity, with her bracing voice, said, "I can't do this. I can't honestly say that I am 100 percent committed to this relationship. I'm sorry."

We were all silent for a long time, staring out at the dusk. "Is there more champagne?" Marcia whimpered.

"She should go easy," Maxine said.

"'She' can make her own decisions," Marcia said. "What are you guys bickering about, anyway? I hate it when you bicker."

Marcia held out her bathroom glass and I refilled it.

"They're arguing about sumptuousness." I held the appetizer plate out to Viola, who was sitting on the end of the bed near my armchair. "Want the last piece of salmon?" Her finger overlapped mine as she took the plate.

"Yum," she said, rolling up the moist raw salmon and placing it on her tongue. With her mouth full, she said, "Oh Maxine! I'm sorry. Did you want some?"

"No."

"So," I said, "how do you fight about sumptuousness? One is for it and the other against it?"

"Do you mind, Bonnie?" This, of course, was Maxine. "It's private."

"It's different interpretations of what is sumptuous," Viola told me.

"I'd like a sumptuous dinner," I said. "These appetizers were dee-lish, but they're all I've had today. Isn't there a fancy-schmancy restaurant attached to this place?" I looked at Marcia and she nodded. "What say I run over and get a menu. I'll bring it back and we can order room service?" All of which would be charged to Carrie's credit card.

"Are we staying the night?" Marcia asked.

"After all this champagne, I should say so."

"I've hardly had any," Maxine said. "I could drive us home."

Everyone ignored her. Mrs. Michaelson said she thought she'd try out that hot tub while I got the menu and ordered dinner. "Steak for me. Well done," she said and disappeared into the bathroom. Viola offered to walk to the restaurant with me. Maxine piped up that she'd come too.

"And leave Marcia alone?" I said.

"Don't leave me alone," Marcia begged.

I nodded at Maxine and left with Viola. Now that the sun had set the air was surprisingly cold. It had a nice salty flavor. Viola said, "So you two, you and Marcia, you were together in high school, no?"

"Yeah," I laughed.

"That's cute. Have you ever, you know, done it for old times' sake?"

"Nah."

"Do you think you'll ever get together again?"

Her questions made me shy. "Unlikely."

"Come on. Tell the truth." Viola nudged me with her elbow and lost her balance, falling into me. "Sorry," she said. "Lots of champagne. Come on, do you think you'd like to get back together with Marcia sometime?"

There was no easy answer to that. It was like an unfinished dream. Who didn't still want what she longed for at eighteen? Feelings born in adolescence maintain a kind of inevitability. The idea of making love with my high school flame, thirty years later, was hot as a fantasy. Just crossing that psychic, emotional, and intellectual distance, just the road itself, was hot. Yet in real life I knew that Marcia was too sweet, too naive for me. "Nah," I said again. "We were kids."

At the restaurant Viola and I got into a giggling fit over the menu. We both wanted sea bass on a fava bean ragout, which struck us as very funny. We decided to just order for everyone to save time. Mrs. Michaelson said she wanted a steak, Viola said she knew that Maxine would want the veggie risotto, and we figured we'd be lucky to get Marcia to eat a little pasta. I ordered more wine, some roasted and marinated sweet pepper crostini appetizers, and a couple of slabs of double fudge chocolate cake to share for dessert, told the maitre d' to have the dinner delivered to the honeymoon suite, and we left, still giggling, because they would think all this food, not to mention the bottles of champagne, was for two people. When the dinner arrived, I lit all the candles in the suite, and everyone but Marcia dug in with ravenous appetites.

"For such a thin girl, you can really pack it away, Max," I told her.

"I work out a lot," she said, as her eyes flitted over my body. I felt as if she were counting the rolls of fat. She added, "Please call me Maxine." Then she turned to Viola. "Hon, wanna try out that hot tub?"

I watched Viola answer. First she looked briefly confused. Then a look of vulnerability crossed her face, followed by resolve. Finally, shyly, "Okay."

When we finished eating, Mrs. Michaelson and I piled the trays outside the door. Viola and Maxine locked themselves in the bathroom.

"I'm going to bed," Mrs. Michaelson announced.

"One bed," Marcia said. "How is this going to work?"

"We're going to use a system called seniority. Though you're welcome to share the bed with me, dear." She crawled in next to her daughter. "Good night, girls."

"Mom, would you please not call us girls? We're pushing fifty."

"Mm-hm. Enjoy your youth." Mrs. Michaelson burrowed under the plush goosedown comforter.

"Ever since Daddy died, she's been this way," Marcia said loudly.

"Uppity."

"I hope it doesn't take you as long as it took me, dear." Within five minutes, she was snoring gently. I sat in my armchair, staring out into the blackness of the night, and strained my ears trying to hear what was going on in the hot tub. I heard a little splashing, but otherwise a strange silence. Could sex be that silent?

Marcia, who hadn't touched dinner but had had plenty of champagne, climbed out of the bed and came to sit on the arm of my chair, leaning into me.

"I love you so much, Bonnie."

"I love you too."

A sudden splash in the bathroom. Like a big fish flopping over.

"What would I do without you?" Marcia asked.

"You wouldn't have made it this far. But you'd be a lot better off if you listened to me more."

"You're right. I'll listen to you from now on. I'll do everything you tell me." Her fingers ran through my hair. "Move over. I want in that chair with you."

Against my better judgment, I squeezed myself into one side of the chair. She slipped off the arm and snuggled in against me, pressing her head into the hollow of my neck. The white terrycloth robe gaped open, revealing her breasts and belly. She smelled both sweet, like baby powder, and sour, like too much champagne.

"Bonnie?" She struggled up and put a finger on my mouth, ran it around the circumference of my lips.

"What do you think Viola and Max are doing?" I asked.

"I don't know," she said. "Don't worry about them."

She kissed me. It was like being eighteen. It was like poetry on her bedroom floor, Friday nights, the threat of being discovered by parents, the fear of separation after graduation. It was the first kiss I'd had in three years. Her mother was asleep, those other two were busy. My hand rested on her hip, inside the robe, slid up her waist. Marcia muttered, "Old times' sake," and tried to kiss me again.

"Honey," I said, straightening up, "it's time for you to go to bed."

"With you," she slurred.

"With your mother."

"I want you."

I extricated myself from the chair and stood looking at my first girlfriend, my oldest friend, slumped there alone. Her second attempt at marriage having failed, just hours after being cast off by her girlfriend, when she was drunk on her butt, she wanted me. It didn't make me angry, but it did make me a little sad. Was I a last resort? Good old faithful Bonnie?

"I'll put you in bed," I said.

"Does that mean no?"

She was more coherent than I had thought.

"That means no." I picked her up, one arm under her shoulders and the other under her knees, and carried her to the bed, where I laid her down.

"Aren't you going to take this robe off of me?"

I stood for a moment beside the bed and looked at her, catching my breath. Wondering. Deciding. Someone pulled the plug in the hot tub and the water began draining with a loud gurgle.

"Goodnight, sweetheart," I said and pulled the covers up over Marcia, leaving her in the opened bathrobe. I kissed her on the lips. I knew she didn't mean any harm. Then, before I had to face the hot tub couple, I found an extra blanket and pillow in the closet and lay down on the floor beside the bed, next to and below Marcia, wondering if I would ever sleep. I heard the bathroom door open, heard scuttling and whispering as Maxine said, "I have sleeping bags in my truck." She would. She went out to get them, and when she returned, I listened to them shake out the bags and spread them on the floor.

For what seemed like hours, I listened to everyone breathe. Marcia was sound asleep, breathing evenly, sweetly. Her mother snored. Someone on the floor, either Viola or Maxine, turned over noisily every few minutes, sighing, obviously as unable to get comfortable as I was. When I could stand it no more, I sat up and read the lit display on the clock next to the bed. Four in the morning. I must have dozed some, but I sure felt like shit. And I needed air. Maxine was right, after all. Staying here was a bad idea.

Quietly I got up and crept out to my car, where I found the fresh pair of jeans and clean shirt I had brought to change into after the wedding. Back in the honeymoon suite, I locked myself in the bathroom and took a long hot shower. I changed into my fresh clothes, then slipped outside again. The ocean air smelled sexy. It was a black night, no moon, and the stars filled the sky. I flopped down on the perfectly manicured green lawn and put my hands behind my head. Clean body, fresh air. I felt a lot better.

"Hey."

I was startled to my feet.

"It's just me. Viola."

"Oh. Hey. You scared me."

"What are you doing out here?" She took my hand and pulled me back down onto the grass.

"Looking at the stars. Waiting until we can go home."

"I couldn't sleep."

"That was you tossing and turning?"

"Yeah. It's too hard on the floor. Maxine can sleep on granite."

"I'd think after your long hot tub, you would sleep well."

Viola looked at me carefully. "What's that supposed to mean?"

The band that held her hair in a ponytail had slipped to the ends of her hair, and most of it hung messily around her face. She wore a T-shirt, no bra, and boxer shorts. The starlight was bright enough for me to see the dark stubble on her legs that hadn't been shaved in a couple of days. "Most people sleep good after sex."

"Huh!" she said. "So that's what you think was happening in the hot tub."

"What? All that silence was meditation?"

"Maxine thought sex would be inappropriate under the circumstances."

"I thought that was why she invited you into the hot tub."

"Me too. I should have known better."

I listened to the waves lapping, now quietly, at the bottom of the cliffs.

"Bonnie, we broke up. Me and Maxine broke up in the hot tub."

"You're not serious?"

"I'm very serious. And I feel as if I have just set down a hundred-pound load. Like I can't imagine why I thought I had to keep carrying it."

"Why did you?"

She shook her head.

"You broke up over sumptuousness?"

She smiled and slapped my thigh. "In a way, yes. Sex. And all that it represents."

"You didn't like sex with Max?"

"What sex?"

"You didn't have sex?"

"About twice in two years…I'm perfectly serious."

My silence must have surprised her. "What?" she said. "You think I'm totally sicko for staying in the relationship? For living without sex?"

I shook my head. "No, babe. I haven't had sex in three years. Not even two perfunctory times like you've had."

"You?" she said as if I were the hottest thing she'd ever seen. Like she'd expect me to be having sex every night with multiple partners.

"Get real," I said, even though I enjoyed the compliment of her tone. "You're good friends with Marcia. I know she's told you my story, at least her interpretation of my story. You know I haven't been with anyone."

"Well, yeah, I did know that." She clasped her knees to her chest. "But that doesn't mean it makes any better sense to me."

Knowing that sitting beside me, alone in the night on a cliff above the sea, was a woman who was apparently as hungry for sex as I was made me feel sad. Because it was never simple. In fact, it was always complicated. I thought of toned, tanned, trim Maxine. Not to mention *young* Maxine. She and I couldn't be more different types, and if that's what Viola liked, well then.

"I'm sure I'm numb," she said. "I'll feel grief later. But right now I'm just relieved it's finally over. Do you know how it feels to fight with someone about whether or not they want you?" She lay back on the grass. "This air feels good. You know, besides breaking up with Maxine"—she snorted a laugh—"besides that, tonight was perfect. I haven't let go like that in a long time. Everyone getting drunk. Eating too much rich food. Laughing. I mean, I hate how hurt Marcia is, but somehow this whole day and night has been a relief."

I nodded, feeling so un-butch, so shy. What happened to the me who invited Sarah Ann to fuck in the supply closet at work? The me who, for that matter, was brazenly flirting with Viola at the wedding just a few hours ago?

"So," she said, "you're a big-shot lawyer, right?"

"Not such a big shot."

"Marcia says you make a lot of money."

"I do."

"She also says you give most of it away."

"I spend plenty. I got that Cherokee. I like nice restaurants."

"Yeah?" she said, getting up on her elbow.

"Yeah," I said, feeling more and more out of control. There is that moment with femmes when you realize that they are in charge, not you, and it's a very uncomfortable feeling. She said, "Can we talk more about why you haven't had sex in three years?"

"Do we have to?"

"No. I'll tell you more about me then. Maxine thinks I'm too wild. She likes very vanilla sex."

"Meaning?"

Viola smiled, enjoying my taking the bait. "Meaning that she likes quiet sex. She likes what she calls 'subtle' sex."

"Why did you stay with her if you didn't like the sex even when you had it?"

"In the beginning we were hot for each other. You know how it is. There's that something that transcends everything reasonable. But she sort of pulled out before I was over the panting phase. So I guess I just never quite realized that it wasn't perfect anyway. Or even close to perfect."

I felt very quiet, wishing Viola hadn't been into Maxine, wondering what it said about her character. But when she asked, "Do you think I'm stupid for being in a relationship like that?" I answered, "Are you kidding. With the stupid relationships I've been in?"

"Bonnie."

"Hm?"

"Am I correct in thinking you've been flirting with me for a good year or more?"

When I couldn't answer because of shyness, she said, "Just nod yes or shake no."

I nodded yes.

"Did you mean it? The flirting?"

I nodded yes again.

"Then will you kiss me now?"

I felt as if some monster of the night leapt on me from behind and held me in place. I couldn't move. I felt scared. Scared like I'd never felt scared before. I hugged my knees and looked out into the blackness over the sea. Her hand moved into the short hair at the back of my head, brushed down my neck, reached around to take hold of my jaw, and gently turned my face toward hers. She put her mouth on mine and kissed me. Kissed me exactly how I liked to be kissed. I was afraid. Afraid of flying apart if she kept this up. Afraid of doing something inappropriate like crying. She pulled me down onto the ground next to her. "Lie on top of me," she demanded, that fast. I was still afraid. My mind wouldn't shut off. What if I crushed her? What was vanilla and what wasn't? What if I was too subtle, like Maxine? What if she was too loud? What if she wanted me to throw her around?

Viola begged me again to lie on top of her, then didn't wait for me to take action. She scooted her body under me and spread her legs. I held her wrists to the ground, over her head, and kissed her harder. My last rational thought was: nearly fifty years old, nearly two hundred pounds, and from all appearances Viola Mendoza was very, very happy with every year and every pound. My brain finally shut off and I'm pretty sure whatever we did wasn't quiet and wasn't subtle, probably wasn't vanilla. Whatever it was, it was good. Too good. Unbearably good. The next part I can remember is laughing about the place where we'd worn some of the grass down to mud. Our clothes were wadded at our feet and I put my hand on Viola again, then took it away right before she came. "What!" she cried. "What are you doing?!"

"Promise you'll never ask me to marry you."

"Oh God, never! I promise." She grabbed my hand and put it back on her. "Never," she said, and came. I rolled on top of her again and she wrapped her legs around my waist, began rocking.

Someone nearby, not me nor Viola, exhaled loudly.

Viola and I froze in our compromised position. Footsteps retreated quickly and the door to the honeymoon suite opened and slammed shut. Viola and I rolled apart, our eyes wide with ecstasy and fright.

We hauled on our clothes. It could have been only one of three people—Maxine, Marcia, or Mrs. Michaelson—and none of them would be happy with what she just saw.

But once dressed, I couldn't sustain feelings of fear or guilt. Viola and I sat side by side, our shoulders pressed together, breathing in unison as we looked out at the sea shimmering silver in the earliest light of dawn. I thought of Marcia's painstakingly crafted wedding vows, the overwrought honeymoon suite, the ironclad expectations of family and friends. How all of this was ruled by a muscular propriety that had, time and again, wrestled genuine love and joy to the ground.

Compare all that to Viola's word—*sumptuous*—a word that conjured the wet, salty air, the grass stains on our skin, the flush feeling in my mouth and breasts, the contents of the ocean before us, teeming, alive, mysterious, unknowable.

Was it even a real choice?

ROAD MAPS

NISA DONNELLY

That year, summer hung green and heavy as guilt over the landing, lulling everything in its path to sleep, to dream, to remember. Mosquitoes glutted with their ill-gotten bounty hovered low and brazen; slap one and see guts of freshly stolen but not-yet-digested blood. They would've carried death in years past, might still, if it weren't for the miracle drugs. Antibiotics.

Wandalee lit a candle, heavy with the smell of camphor, its yellow flame dancing slow against the oncoming night, the way the moon sometimes appeared to dance on the river. The camphor was supposed to send the bugs a warning, and perhaps it did, although river bugs are hardy and not easily scared. And less easily moved. River bugs, river rats. *Drive a knife in him and you'd get mud not blood.* The old-timers like Wandalee's granddaddy, the Devil, used to say that and laugh. Only they weren't talking about bugs or rats so much as they were describing themselves.

Night was sliding over the river then, making its way down along the highway where a pair of headlights skimmed without slowing, the pale glow bouncing off the sign that offered fried river cats and cold beer.

CO D BEER, really. The L had fallen off sometime during last winter's storms. She'd have to get one of those nasty Horace boys from town out to fix it. That'd cost her. Last time they spent two days drinking her beer and making jokes about the nudes over the bar, all for an hour of sign painting. Not that it was all that easy to get one of them to come out. Wasn't like in the old days when the Devil's Landing was a place people wanted to come. Now it was just a place. Every year fewer travelers turned down the blacktop leading to the landing, and fewer locals too, for that matter, with the exception of the duck hunters in winter and the fishermen in summer, or sometimes them and the rich city men who paid them to be taken out on the river. The cars seldom slowed, heading instead toward the McDonald's and Wendy's in the towns at either end of the highway.

Wandalee and Mazie understood the need for sameness; didn't they look for it themselves when they took the travel trailer over to Branston or down to Memphis, or that one time out to the Grand Canyon? She couldn't remember a single blacktop they'd turned down, following a sign for fried cats or cold beer or anything else. Yes, with McDonald's and Wendy's you know what to expect, whether you're in Missouri or Tennessee or Arizona. There's a certain comfort in that, a certain healing sameness.

Which is why they were surprised when the girls came, trailing down the road like a pair of lost pups. Not many new faces found their way down the highway, almost none down their blacktop, and none that she could ever remember with New Jersey license plates and accents like something off a television comedy show. Wandalee brought them in, aiming to keep them from the very start. Mazie may have suspected, but hadn't yet accused. Forty years they'd been planning to go to California: forty years of watching summer turn into fall and fall into rain then ice then rain again then summer. Forty years of promises broken and neglected and sometimes just forgotten knit together into their life. Finally, Wandalee had understood: the ghosts would never let her go unless.... She'd sat up in bed the night she knew it to be true, her heart pounding, sure that Mazie could hear the roar in her chest. *Unless there was someone else.* The ghosts had sent her Mazie after the war—hadn't she been planning on leaving then? They'd conspired to keep the pair of them here, tending to the past, marking time. "Oh, God." Mazie had snored loudly, her hand reaching automatically to caress Wandalee's plump left thigh. "Oh, God."

And then the girls had come. Wandalee had willed them here, she was sure of that, although she told no one. Mazie, though, knew them for what they were: followers, rounders, lost souls looking for someplace to belong because the place they really did belong had stopped suiting them. She didn't know why, didn't really care, but she knew the look of the lost, the way their eyes darted, missing nothing and at the same time seeing nothing, the way their fingers drum-drummed against the tabletop, tapping out questions and aimless percussion to unsung melodies; knew it because she'd seen that look in her own mirror, silenced her own fingers; knew it because Wandalee had brought her in, too, and kept her, the willing accomplice, until life had washed across them both the way the river washed out of its banks every spring and sometimes in the winter, too.

They were old women now. Mazie could no longer remember what it was like to have been young, and Wandalee could not forget the girls they'd been. And now, for whatever reason, ghosts or enterprise, it didn't really matter, there were two more watching the days turn into weeks and, lately, months. Maybe Wandalee was right, maybe they would find a way to stay, to claim the landing, to set Mazie and Wandalee free. If it was possible, then it surely was time.

Mazie was whisper-singing as she tinkered with the aging engine that had brought Kris and Shelly down the blacktop to the landing. Leaning against the old gas pump, Kris watched Mazie work. It was true: Mazie spent more time talking to engines than to people. Easy to imagine how the two women had existed together for so many years: Wandalee gabbing like a meth-addicted crow and Mazie nodding, her eyes half closed, pretending to listen but really thinking of carburetors and cams. With the hood hiding so much of Mazie's face, it was possible to imagine what she might have been like young, before the years settled, leaving her skin like a piece of leather out too long in the weather. How old must she be—sixty? No, more like seventy, Kris decided, trying to make the song Mazie kept singing under her breath familiar, and failing.

> *Margie had some marmalade,*
> *Margie had some beer,*
> *Margie had some other things,*
> *That made her feel so queer,*
> *Whoops! went the marmalade,*
> *Whoops! went the beer,*
> *Whoops! went the other things,*
> *That made her feel so queer.*

"Mazie, what's the name of that song?"

Mazie turned, smiled. Gold flashed from the right side of her mouth, giving the appearance of a crooked grin. "Don't know that it has one. If it does, I never heard it. Just something my mama used to sing. Why you ask?"

"Just…I don't know, it makes me remember…something from a long time ago." Kris rubbed her wrist.

The old woman looked, nodded, went back to her tinkering, her singing.

KRIS, 1968

For fifteen years, from the time I was six years old, I wore a bracelet of scars that I called pearls. Ten, perfectly round at first, that stretched wide and then wider until no longer round, no longer perfect, they grew with every season, fading with each year that passed. Until finally they stretched so far or thin or wide that they resembled a ribbon, a rubberband, a bit of twine more than pearls. And then, one day, they were gone. Like Margie, the girl who'd put them there.

My mother hated Margie. Or maybe not. Maybe it was fear. Maybe she saw her own misshapen past in that child who squatted next to the back steps waiting for me to be released from lunch. "What'dya eat?" Margie was picking the scab on her left knee that never seemed to heal. She didn't look anyone in the eye when she talked, or at any other time that I can remember.

"Dunno." Food repulsed me. I was sick that year, with a rare anemia that the doctors had misdiagnosed as leukemia, but we wouldn't know that yet for months. Whatever was wrong had kept me out of school since March and promised to keep me out again for the foreseeable future. Just before my diagnosis, my parents had come to live with my grandmother in the old family place between fields and orchards outside of town. I'd spent six weeks in Mrs. Cranshaw's fourth grade before my grandmother's doctor banished me to bed. It was hardly enough time to make friends, and my parents apparently saw no reason to find friends for me.

Margie and her brother Carl lived with their father down by the creek in a rundown, two-room cabin that my grandfather had built to get away from his family, which my grandmother now rented out to families who collected general assistance, which meant that the county paid her the rent. Of course, I wasn't supposed to know any of that. Margie was the only other child in a two-mile radius; Carl, at thirteen, was technically not a child. I seldom saw him.

"Apples? Did'ya eat apples? I like apples. Yellow ones. I like yellow apples best. I bet you ate yellow apples." Margie's voice spun higher and faster as her grubby fingers worked the scab. "An...what else? What else you eat, huh?" Margie freed the scab, scraped it off onto her bottom front teeth and chewed deliberately. She reminded me of a rabbit. Satisfied, she bent down and gently licked the droplets of blood, looked up at me, angry, grabbed my upper arm. "I said—what else you eat?"

My arm was already darkening—I bruised easily. But then, I was dying, everybody said so, and I had no reason not to believe them. I tried to shake her off, but her fingers only dug in more deeply.

Paradise could be had for a quarter in the summer of 1968. And, thanks to my father's misplaced guilt and the misdiagnosis of a near-sighted octogenarian, quarters puddled into silvery ponds, illuminated by the faint light of a crusting mirror that leaned against the wall behind the ancient vanity table in Granny's front bedroom, which was now my room. The table, painted pink by my daddy for his baby sister Kristina, who died way before I was born, had faded to a dirty beige. Except for the backs of the legs, where bright pink drooled and bubbled, a testament to my father's boyish ineptitude with a paint brush. Flamingoes, white with orange-blushed wings, stood one-legged in a foggy gray marsh. I had never seen a flamingo, so it didn't occur to me until years later when we were cleaning out my grandmother's house that the flamingoes must have once been pink, too.

The sight of Auntie Kristi, lips puckered as if she'd been eating lemons, eyes fixed on something that only she could see, greeted me every morning from the corner of that dressing table, where sticky bottles of dried-up cologne stood like tiny, misshapen sentinels awaiting their queen who'd run off at sixteen to marry a sailor from Lexington and ended up drowned in a deep but narrow place in the Wabash River.

The sailor came to the house afterward to tell how it had happened. How they'd had a flat tire on a stretch of back road where the bridge was narrow. He'd jacked the car up, telling Auntie Kristi to stay inside because it was dark and he was a gentleman, and just as he was giving it the final lift with the jack, the side of the bridge started to give way and the car tumbled over, twenty feet down to the water. He'd heard the car hit the water, sure, but the moon was dark. He'd dived in after her, calling her name, pushing himself under the black water, until the river nearly claimed him as well. He'd made his way to the bank, somehow, he must have because wasn't that where he came to at dawn, too late to do more. Surely the family understood. There was nothing more he or providence could have done. Or so he said, my father would intone whenever he recalled that sailor's visit.

The next morning, the sheriff's office in that county three states away had pulled the Oldsmobile Cutlass convertible to the surface, top torn away, without Auntie Kristi. It had taken the rest of the day to find her, her legs entangled in the branches of a sunken tree, as if she'd tried to swim to shore, but had been caught along the way, a large bruise on the side of her face. The sailor had come right away to tell the family; it was the honorable thing to do, he said.

My father called the man an idiot, a coward, a murderer. His story didn't make sense, he'd raged. *That boy would pay for his sins, whether they be the result of cowardice, stupidity, or malice. He would kill the sonofabitch himself, blow his brains out just for the pleasure of watching the blood splatter, gladly go to the electric chair for the joy of seeing the little runt dead, only no jury on earth would convict him.* "Dead! You'd be better off dead!" my father had shouted from the porch as the man scurried into the night, never to be seen again.

"I should've shot him when I had the chance," he would say over and over, whenever his thoughts turned to that night, as they often did when he was drinking.

Of course, I wasn't close to being around when all this happened. My mother, who was Kristi's best friend, settled her grief and tried to settle my father's by naming me for the dead girl who'd run away with a coward-idiot-murderer in the name of love. I was pretty sure I wouldn't do anything that stupid. Margie, on the other hand, insisted that marrying for love was almost as good as marrying for money. I wasn't sure how she'd know. Money was about the only thing that mattered to Margie.

I twisted my arm loose, but she caught me again.

"Let go, Margie." She pushed her narrow, fox-like face close to mine. Dust streaks ran from her cheek into her uncombed, unwashed hair, which she occasionally ploughed with her fingers.

"What'll you give me if I do?"

"A quarter," I sighed. It was always the same. A quarter for my freedom. I dug it out of my jeans. What did it matter? There seemed to be an endless supply of quarters in the little green dish next to Auntie Kristi's picture.

"You wanna play a game, Kris-teeeee?"

I cringed. Nobody ever called me anything other than Kris, as if they couldn't stand to hear the sound of her name, even after they'd named me for her. Margie had already pocketed the quarter and released my arm. Sure enough, four finger-sized welts were beginning to show.

"It's a game my brother showed me. You get it right—it's worth this dollar and more. 'Course, you lose, you pay." She was dancing from one foot to the other; it was hard to tell if Margie had to pee or if she was merely excited at the prospect of winning.

I glanced back toward the house. Mama and Granny wouldn't be looking for me for another hour. I checked the sun. It was nearly one o'clock by my estimate. That meant another hour of freedom before the iron treatments and the forced nap. Nobody cared that I couldn't sleep while the sun was up, just as they didn't care that the iron treatment made me feel like I was going to heave all over Granny's shiny black oxfords that she only laced up when she went to church.

"A dollar? You don't even have a dollar, Margie."

"Do so." Margie grinned, wriggled one grubby foot out of its shoe, and began digging diligently in the toe of the canvas sneaker. Sure enough, she produced a dollar bill, wrinkled and obviously well-used, but a dollar bill nonetheless.

"I got it off Carl." Her voice was almost a whisper. Carl was danger and evil personified into the person of one gangly, somewhat larger version of Margie. Carl smoked stolen cigarettes and shoplifted bags of chocolate drops and jelly beans from Newberry's for me and Margie. He called it boosting, which Margie insisted wasn't the same as stealing. Boosting was just helping yourself to what you needed that everybody had too much of to keep track of anyway. I wasn't certain I believed her, although the jelly beans didn't taste stolen, I had to admit that. And sinful candy surely couldn't taste the same.

"He don't know I got it. I boosted it when he wasn't looking. Now it's mine. What you got to put up against it?"

I hesitated.

"I know." Margie was grinning again. "That little old transistor radio of yours ought to cover it."

Now I knew for sure I was being set up. Margie had coveted that radio from the first time she'd seen it. No larger than a package of cigarettes, it was in a genuine leather case, white, and had a little earplug attached so that you could carry it in your pocket and still listen with nobody being the wiser, as long as they didn't notice the earplug, of course. So far, Granny had always spotted the earplug every time I tried wearing it in church.

I shook my head.

Margie shrugged. "Okay, so you're a yellow-bellied coward. That's okay. I didn't figure you were tough enough to play a game like this one anyway, it being such high stakes and all, but I figured I'd give you the chance." She stuffed her foot back into the shoe. "Well, see you." As she was walking away, she suddenly whirled back at me, her fingers tucked into her armpits, and flapped and cackled like a chicken.

I don't remember how I came to knock her to the ground, only that I did—that and the sense of exhilaration that came with the attack. I was hitting and biting and kicking and rolling in the dirt and what's more, I was winning. Pulling back, Margie shook her head as if she couldn't quite believe what had happened.

"Take it back." I balled my fist the way I'd seen my boy cousins do. "Unless you want more of this, take it back."

Margie leaned back on her haunches, considering. "You'll play the game?"

"You'll take it back?"

"Okay, I take it back. Now, you got to play the game."

I followed her to the potting shed, back beyond the old maple tree where Granny kept the lawn mower and garden tools. Inside the shed smelled of earth and secrets. Margie gave the old whetting wheel a spin. It had been my grandfather's, although no one had used it in my memory, my father preferring to take the garden implements to the hardware store in town whenever they needed an edge put back on. It stood next to the window, making crazy patterns on the wavy glass when the wheel spun fast enough. Margie cranked the old wheel once, twice, three times, until it was spinning nearly out of control, then held her fingers just above it, drawing them back if the wheel wobbled too close. If her fingers had been iron, sparks would have snapped against the gloom. The wheel slowed and Margie sighed, dropping onto a burlap potato sack stuffed with straw. She looked like a scrawny bird sitting on its nest.

"You got a cig?" She knew I didn't. Nobody in my family smoked, but she always asked. I shook my head as she produced a worn pack that was carefully folded to protect its lone cigarette, only slightly smoked, and a pair of stick matches. Contraband from Carl, I assumed. Nobody would sell an eight-year-old kid one cigarette. Even I knew that. She struck the match against the wheel and lit the cigarette, inhaling slowly. "Want some?" She extended it toward me. I shook my head, trying to look nonchalant, and wondered what I was supposed to do if my grandmother—What-in-the-name-of-sweet-Jesus-is-that-I-smell?—detected cigarette smoke in her garden shed, or worse, on me? I backed closer to the door, opening it a little.

"Come on over here," Margie commanded. "You can't play from over there."

I dropped down next to her on the bags, pulling my knees up under my chin, curious.

"Okay, now here's how we do it. I bet your transistor radio against this dollar and my—what do you want of mine? I know, my repeater rifle. That's worth a fair amount. Okay, this dollar and my repeater rifle says that I can't set fire to this dollar bill in ten tries using this cigarette before you tell me to stop. 'Course, if you tell me to stop you got to pay me with that radio. Okay?"

I didn't want the repeater rifle. It was a cheap plastic toy that didn't work half the time. Besides, it was a stupid bet. Everybody knew that money burns.

"What's the matter? You going chicken on me again?"

I looked at Margie, her eyes shining with excitement. She was about to start that wiggling she had done before, when I said, "Okay," surprising even myself.

Margie was grinning. "Now hold out your wrist," she told me.

I did so, grudgingly.

Margie grabbed my forearm and wrapped the dollar bill around my wrist, tightly. Her eyes flashed evil, but she was smiling almost sweetly.

"Ready?" Without waiting for a reply, she held the burning cigarette against the green paper. It smoked, but didn't light. I inhaled sharply, looked in Margie's eyes, then up at the ceiling. "One Mississippi," she said.

By the time Margie got to ten Mississippi, I had floated far away, hovering near the ceiling of the potting shed, near the bottom of the river where Auntie Kristi breathed water, near the door of my hospital room where my mother cried every time the doctor said "leukemia." I was soaring and strong and free. Nothing could hurt me, if I didn't let it. I hadn't said a word.

"Well, I'll be goose damned," said Margie as she pulled the dollar bill away.

Blisters were already rising on my wrist. Pearls, I thought, looking at them; they looked like red pearls. "I'll be goose damned," she repeated, almost as a whisper, reaching out to touch them gingerly or perhaps reverently, I've never quite known. That's when I saw the evidence on her wrist: two perfect circles and one lighter. She'd cried uncle. She'd lost and I'd won. I'd won twice in the same afternoon. I wanted to gloat, to sing, *Who's the yellow-belly now?*, but something in the way Margie looked when she pulled her wrist back, when she knew I'd seen, stopped me.

"I've got to go in now, Margie. It's time for my treatment." I held out my hand for the dollar. Grudgingly, she extended it. I stuffed it into my pocket. "Bring the repeater by later?"

She nodded, and I pretended not to notice the fat tear that trembled down her cheek, hanging on her chin, before it dropped onto her grubby shirt.

"You come over after supper and I'll bring you out a piece of Granny's lemon cake."

No response.

"Well, I got to go in now," I repeated, turning my back as Margie started the wheel to spinning again.

My grandmother, cluck-clucking, dressed my wrist in her special concoction of burn cream. My mother threatened to beat me within an inch of my life if I ever did anything like that again, and then burst into tears; I guess it's hard to hit a child when you think she's dying of leukemia. It took Margie two days, but she finally brought the repeater over. It was in worse shape than I'd imagined, and I let her have it back after a couple of days of trying to get it to work. It just didn't seem to be worth the trouble.

That fall, a blood specialist who was giving a lecture at the university near the hospital where I was being treated took an interest in my case. I'd become a bit of a celebrity because I'd shown no signs of the disease advancing. He discovered that not only was I not dying, but that I had a blood disease that was only beginning to be understood and showed every evidence of responding to treatment. The months of ill-prescribed treatments by Granny's doctor had left me considerably weakened, but the prognosis was excellent, the expert said; I could expect to lead a long and normal life. I've since suspected that his definition of normal and mine are considerably different.

My grandmother declared my recovery to be a miracle and called Brother Steve, the local evangelist who hosted the *Hour of Power* radio program, where followers had been praying for me for the last eight months. Brother Steve even came to the hospital and devoted a whole show to my cure. Nobody mentioned the blood specialist from Chicago.

By the time I got back from the hospital and my brush with fame, Margie no longer lived there. I overheard Granny telling my mother that Margie's dad hadn't been seen in weeks, and that a social worker had finally come for Margie and Carl, who had fought like a wild animal—it took two men to get him into the car before it was over. During the ruckus, Margie had disappeared, but they'd found her in the potting shed when Granny had heard the whetting wheel spinning. She was cranking that wheel as fast as it would go, holding her fingernails against it. All but two of the nails had been ripped off and bled through. Margie'd gone quietly enough in the end, though.

I went out to the potting shed to see if she'd left anything for me. I don't know what I expected. A note, maybe, or her old plastic repeater, or even a quarter, or a half-smoked cigarette. But there wasn't a thing there that hadn't always been in the shed, just a few rust-colored streaks on that old wheel, and for all I know, they could've been there for a long, long time.

MAZIE, 1992

The river remembers. Not everyone can understand its garbled songs, and some who can pretend they can't. To Wandalee, it's her granddaddy and his friends, laughing and dancing on that barge they kept anchored off shore. I've tried, but what she insists are the sounds of glasses tinkling seem like nothing more to me than chain lapping up against Richard Darling's johnboat; women laughing, birds calling to the full moon. But then, I have my own memories, ones that the river never knew. Still, I hear it lapping out the same story, my story, over and over again, taking me back. I lie awake some nights listening to it, waiting for it to make a mistake, to leave something out. It never does. Should I take comfort in that, knowing that whenever I start to forget, all I have to do is listen and the river will tell me?

Big dicks and small brains. That's the problem with most of the men I've met. Not my uncles, though. They were smart and well-hung, at least that's what they told each other. Maybe it was true, maybe not. I can attest to the one, wouldn't have a clue about the other—never saw a one of them naked. They were careful about things like that. Maybe they thought I'd seen enough naked men to last me a lifetime, and they were right.

My mother wasn't much in the way of brains. Nobody said anything, they didn't have to; it was just something you knew. But pretty? That woman could have stopped traffic on 42nd Street, if you know what I mean. She was little, not like me. I take after my daddy, I suppose, even though I never knew him. He was an army mule. That's what they called men like him in those days. He was dark, I know that, and big, I reckon, although it's hard to tell how big a man truly is from a head-and-shoulders photograph.

Mama married him on the front porch of the county jail. The sheriff was also a justice of the peace, and he conducted most of his weddings on the porch unless it was raining. Rain meant you got the jail cells as a backdrop, which wasn't much of a way to start off married life. Mama was fifteen years old, or fourteen or sixteen depending on when she was telling the story. As I said, she wasn't much in the way of brains. Her brothers, my uncles, arrived just as the happy couple had said their I do's. *They* weren't happy about that, I can tell you. My uncles had planned to stop the wedding—or barring that, take turns beating some sense into the bridegroom—because my mama was their only sister and they thought she deserved better than some army mule who was half Mexican and half Indian, which means a whole lot of half nothing in the part of the world where I grew up, just outside of El Paso, Texas.

Now, my mama may not have been book-smart, but she did know that her brothers wouldn't beat anybody, even her new husband, on the porch of the county jail. So she got to take him home in one piece—her brothers would just have to get used to it. As it turned out, her new husband enjoyed beating on my uncles as much as they enjoyed beating on him. It must've been quite a honeymoon. Well, a few months passed like that before they made peace, then I was born, and then he met up with a German landmine and that was the end of him. I never knew him.

It was funny, in a way. Mama never cried. I didn't know that at the time, of course, but my grandmama and my uncles told me about it. How she took the telegram that the army sent and put it under her pillow. Wouldn't read it. Wouldn't let anyone else read it, either. One day passed, then two, then three. They were all waiting around for her to open the telegram. She pretended like it wasn't even there. Went on about her business: gathered eggs in the morning, baked bread in the afternoon, did the wash on Mondays and the ironing on Tuesdays, and nursed me in between her chores. She was organized like that. Finally, after more than a week had passed and she still hadn't opened that telegram, her mama went and got it out from under that pillow, took her pocketknife, and split it open neat as you please. It said what they all knew it would, that my daddy was dead and how it happened and that his personal effects and what was left of him would be arriving directly. Over dinner that night, after they'd said grace, my grandmama took the telegram out of her pocket and had my oldest uncle read it aloud.

My mama still didn't say a thing, just got up from the table and went into her room. When she came out she was wearing her white sharkskin dress with red piping and her matching red high-heeled shoes and the hat with the red veil and white dots, and carrying her little red purse. It was the outfit she'd gotten married in. She didn't say a thing to any of them, walked out the door and down the gravel road that led to town. Her brothers wanted to go after her, but their mama said, "No, let her be. Women got to grieve in their own way. She'll be back."

Instead of coming back, though, she bought a bus ticket to San Diego, where her dead husband had family. They took her in, gave her the three thousand dollars he'd sent his mother to put away for him. Mama used that to buy herself a little house, and she got a job selling millinery in a dress shop that catered to women who weren't looking for a hat to wear to Sunday service, if you know what I mean. Those women took a liking to her. Taught her how to dance and smoke and play cards, none of which my grandmama had allowed. They would've taught her how to dress and make a man feel like a million bucks, too, but some things my mama came by naturally.

I don't think I saw her until I was seven, almost eight years old. I remember it was unseasonably cold out, because when I opened up the kitchen door, my eyeglasses fogged over and I could just barely see the lady sitting at the table with Grandmama. "This here's your mama," she said. "She's come for you." I always thought Grandmama's voice sounded like she was crying, but by the time I got the fog cleared off my glasses she didn't look any different than usual. It was years before I figured out that she'd called my mother to come for me not because Mama wanted me, but because of the cancer that was eating out my grandma's stomach.

"Call me Kate," said my mother.

We rode the bus from Texas to California. Mama made friends with the men who sat in the back of the bus drinking out of paper bags and smoking cigarettes and laughing a lot. She made me sit in the seat just behind the driver. Sometimes at the rest stops, he'd bring me a soda pop from the machine. Sometimes, he forgot. Sometimes Mama and her friends would take me into the restaurants and we'd eat fried egg sandwiches. Mama told people I was her kid sister. That I was ten years old. That it was up to her to take care of me because our folks were dead, killed in a fire, and if not for her I'd be in an orphanage. She told that story so often, I think she actually came to believe it. After a while, even I believed it might be true.

My mother's friends from the shop weren't impressed with me. I suppose they had expected a child-sized version of my mother, not a hulking kid with crooked teeth, kinky hair, and glasses, who had no use for dolls or girlie dresses or lace anklets. The men who came to see Kate didn't seem to care, though. They brought me things. Jawbreakers, mostly, and once a kite that was shaped like a bird. One worked for the railroad and he gave me a whole little train, piece by piece, that you glued together. Another gave me a ship in a bottle. He wanted Kate to marry him, so he was willing to invest a little more in me.

I think I always knew what my mama was. But I wasn't ashamed or shocked. She was just Kate, and Kate was a very friendly woman. She did finally marry one of her men. Lester worked at the shipyards, and if it had an engine, he could repair it. He had some sort of sleeping disorder that came from being in the war—he just didn't sleep. I think maybe he was afraid of what it would bring. Anyway, Les worked all day at the shipyard and most of the night out in the garage. He taught me everything I know about engines. But he died young, probably lack of sleep did him in. That and Kate's drinking.

I don't know why my uncles came out to San Diego. Maybe it was for work, maybe it was because after my grandmother died there just wasn't much left for them back in Texas. But I do know that when they showed up, Kate was having one of her parties. She'd been entertaining more than usual since Lester died. Kate liked young men, and San Diego was full of them. Some of them didn't even look like they were old enough to shave. Some of them couldn't have been much older than me, although it wasn't me they were coming to see. My job was to serve the drinks, clean up the puke, and stay out of the way. I was fourteen, looked twenty, and nobody bothered to think of me as a girl. Not Kate. Not the men who came to see her. Not even me.

Women like Kate don't often come to good ends, but they have one helluva good time getting there. She died that year. One of those sailors had left her with a little memento that she waited too long to get rid of. By the time she got sober enough to think about finding a doctor, she was already five months along. And she lied to the doctor, who wasn't really anything more than an orderly at the veteran's hospital. He said she'd told him three months at the most, or he wouldn't have done it. I don't know if that's true or not. I met a nurse once, though, who told me that the further along a woman is, the more fragile the uterus. I guess the doctor scraped a little too deep or maybe left a piece of that sailor's calling card up inside her. Whatever it was, it killed her. My uncles sent her back to Texas to the family plot and had her put next to my grandmother. Then they went hunting for that doctor.

They found him working at the veteran's hospital. The man didn't even have the good sense to hide. They took his right hand off. Said they would've killed him, but since what he did to Kate wasn't intended, they'd let him off easy. There wasn't any way to know which of the sailors was responsible, of course, so they spent the next six months beating any boy in white who crossed their paths. It helped to pass the time and wear out their grief.

Most girls love their mamas, I know that. Most of them aren't in love with their mamas, I know that, too. But I was. From the first time I saw her, there in Grandmama's kitchen, I was in love with Kate. She was everything to me. Everything I wanted. Everything I couldn't be—but maybe something I could possess. I wanted to own her, to claim her. I wanted her to touch me, to love me, to make me part of her, and she didn't or couldn't, I don't know which. Instead, she told people that I was her sister, as if to say that it was impossible I had once inhabited her perfect body. She looked at me, I suppose, and couldn't imagine that something so big, so ugly could ever have come out of her. And the more I knew that, the more she pulled away, the more I wanted her.

I thought if I did everything right, she would want me. I taught myself how to do all the things she wouldn't or couldn't do herself. I cleaned the house and cooked the food, served the drinks, changed the records on the phonograph without leaving so much as a scratch. She didn't care if I went to school, so I didn't. When the truant officers came around, she would sometimes lie, sometimes not. Mostly, she would let them take me, if they could catch me. I wasn't hers, not really. That's what she told them. What she didn't say, what she didn't have to say, was that hers would have been beautiful, like her: tiny and pink and perfect, like the dolls she kept on her lace bedspread. I knew those dolls. Hated them. Loved them. Loved her.

When Kate saw her brothers at the door that first time, she laughed. One of her men had his hand up inside her skirt. She turned to me and said, "Get your uncles a couple of drinks. What'dya boys want, beer or something stronger?" It was the same voice she used for all her party guests. She wasn't particular what I served; whatever the guests brought was what we had. That was the price of admission, a fifth and flowers or stockings or candy, and always a little help with the rent or the gas bill.

The uncles didn't recognize me. They thought I was a boy from the neighborhood.

"Do they ever touch you?" one of them asked me later, meaning the men who weren't all that much older than me, who would have been calling on me and not my mother if I had been like her, like her dolls. Touch me? They thought I was a boy, not even an attractive boy. I couldn't even catch the eye of the ones who were interested only in boys and who'd come to Kate's because they were ashamed of where they really wanted to be. I was too stocky, too clumsy, too ashamed to meet any man's eye. "No," I said, pretending not to know what the uncles meant, "they come to see Kate."

I never had to ask why the men came. I understood. When Kate laughed, it was like music; when she cried, I would hold her and rock her, brush her hair. I never called her Mama, never thought of her that way. I would kiss her eyes and her forehead, her cheeks where the tears were still salt glistening.

"Don't look at me," she'd say, "I look a mess when I cry." I would pretend to look away, would tell her what she wanted to hear, that she was the most beautiful woman in the world. That I would take care of her no matter what. That she was perfect. To me, it wasn't a lie.

After she died, the girls from the shop started a collection for me. I took that and all the money I could find around the house and caught a bus up the coast to the shipyards in Richmond, just north of San Francisco, where my uncles were working by then. Nobody asked my age. Nobody figured I was anything but a boy. I lived there with my uncles in a little house near the bay. It wasn't a bad way to live. Stayed there until the accident. That left me restless.

You asked me how I come to be here, but you want a better answer than rain and the river. Like rain ain't good enough. How it seeps into the seams along the windshield. How the rain come crawlin' up that glass, hit me in the face, like tears, as if I could remember how to cry, as if I ever knew how. Hell, I never even cried when that hook come loose, when that hunk of steel come at me and crushed my leg, never even cried when they told me they took it off.

I was going on twenty years old and had one whole leg, half of another one, and twenty thousand dollars in settlement money. I was rich and I was crazy. Crazy with grief, crazy with loneliness, crazy with the pain. Some nights I'd wake up screaming, that leg hurt so bad. Just 'cause something's gone, doesn't mean it can't hurt. Phantom pain, is what the doctors call it. I just call it misery. The worst pain I ever had was in that leg, and there is not one damned thing you can do to stop it. Can't rub it away. Can't soak it away. Can't do nothing but wait it out.

I even tried to outrun it. Bought a car, a convertible, fancy car set up so that I could drive it with just the one leg. I took that car from one side of this country to the other, although I never did go back to California. I didn't much care for the cold—it seemed to make the pain in my leg worse—so I spent most of my time where it was warm. Followed the sun, followed the moon, followed the sunrise and the sunset. Finally took to following the rivers. That's how I came to be here with Wandalee.

Oh, she was a wonder. I found her and loved her, and then the pain started up again and I left one night. Never said nothing, just packed up and left at first light. She was still living in the big house by herself and I was still in the cabin, and I thought about leaving a note, but nothing came to mind. I did send her a postcard or two, though. Pictures of places I was traveling through. And when it started to rain—I think I must've been down in New Orleans or thereabouts—I started to remember her and this place. It was as if she was calling to me. She says it was the ghosts, but I don't believe in ghosts or mind reading, none of that. It was the memory of her that was creeping back in with the rain. I kept seeing how she must've cried when she found I was gone without so much as a note, kept imagining her eyes and how they'd look through tears. And it made me sad. If I'd known how to cry, I would've. So I started back. Got lost. I've taken my share of wrong turns in this life, and coming back here was no exception. It took me a while to find my way back to her. I tell her it was because I was on the wrong side of the river, and she knows what I mean. She was here waiting.

It was pouring rain that afternoon, same as it was the first time I drove into this driveway. There's easier things to negotiate in crutches than loose gravel in the rain, I can tell you, but I managed. I went into the bar. A couple of the fishermen were inside playing cards, waiting out the rain. Wandalee was in the kitchen. I could see her through that little window, probably making one of her pies. I was pulling up a chair by one of those back tables when I caught sight of myself in the mirror behind the bar. I wasn't nothing anybody would want—looking like something drowned and dragged in from the river. Maybe should've turned to go, maybe could've made it out without her noticing. But then I saw those two postcards I'd sent, tucked up next to the cash register, and I knew this was a place I was welcome.

"Well, look who's here!" she said, her face shining brighter than any neon in the place. The regulars turned and looked, smiled, nodded, not really recognizing me. "Look who's come home!"

I don't know what brought me back. Could've been pure loneliness. Or love. Sometimes I think it was the river. The old men who've lived around here a long time tell you that the river always comes back to claim its driftwood.

I suppose that's what I am, what you are, too, when you think about it. You can leave, but it'll always bring you back.

SHELLY, 1993

Rivers remember. The old woman told me that the first week we were here. Mazie. Crazy Mazie. Not that I would ever call her that to her face. She'd take a tire iron to my head, or a ratchet. Well, maybe not, but I wouldn't put it past her. She's not sweet the way Wandalee is, although Kris seems to like her better. I can't imagine why.

I keep waiting. Kris keeps putting me off, as if she likes it here. She says it's a good deal, that we can sit out the winter here, save the money we brought with us and put some by—Mazie pays her pretty good for working in the shop. The old women stopped charging us rent after the first week. So long as we're willing to listen to their stories, they seem content to have us around. Lately, Kris works in the garage more than Mazie, at least it seems that way.

Wandalee's teaching me how to bake pies and how to fry channel cats. She says I need a little more practice to get the batter right. Channel cats are catfish caught in the river channels. See, I'm learning something. In the evening, when the old women go up to their house to do whatever it is old women do, I tend bar, talk to the people who come by. They aren't so bad. I'm starting to know the regulars, what they drink, who pays and who runs a tab, who tips and who would rather die than part with a damned quarter. Wandalee says she's grateful for my help. I think it's more that she's grateful for the company. At least I have something to say to her. Mazie just sits and stares. If that woman puts a dozen sentences together in a day, it's something to write home about. Not that I ever do—write home. It's just an expression.

What am I supposed to say? That I fell in love with a woman I hardly knew and without thinking about it, lapped up the idea of running away with her to California? Running away isn't even true, because there was nothing I was running from. Running toward is what I did, or started to do, before we got waylaid here. We were on our way to somewhere and ended up in the middle of nowhere. Nobody I know wants to hear that and even if they did, I don't want them to know the truth: that I took off with the first person who asked. The thing is, I knew there was something better out there, and all I needed to do was find it. I still believe that it's out there, whatever it is that I'm looking for, and that all I have to do is find it.

That's what I mean about Mazie being crazy. She's been all over, met people, really lived, and yet here she sits, talking about the river remembering, and driftwood. And it's not just because she's old; she wasn't so old when she came here. She probably wasn't any older than Kris or me when she and Wandalee met. They should've sold this place when there was still something to sell and taken off for California. Lived a little, not just settled for this.

Hell, what they call a beach is nothing but sticky muck, and what sand there is isn't much better. Every damned time I go near that beach I get stuck. The worst was when I sunk down to my knees and couldn't get out until Kris finally heard me hollering and came to pull me out. Wandalee says I get stuck because I walk too slow, like I'm afraid of something. Damned right I'm afraid: I'm afraid of being sucked down and buried alive.

Once Kris and I get out of here, once we finally get to California, I plan to go and sit on the beach and just feel hot, dry sand for about a week. Then, I'm going to send Wandalee and Mazie a postcard so they'll know what a real beach looks like. I think I'd like to work in a place where there are lots of travelers, where people on their way to somewhere stop by. Maybe in one of those airport shops. You could learn a lot in a place like that: learn where life is good, what other places are like, whether the people are friendly or not. Then, when you end up somewhere, it's not just an accident, or some crummy joke that fate's decided to play on you.

I've got to talk to Kris about leaving. Maybe in the morning, depending on the mood she's in, or the day after at the latest. Well, soon, anyway. I mean, we can't stay here forever, can we?

JOE LOUIS WAS A HECK OF A FIGHTER

Jewelle Gomez

Manhattan lay glittering like a sequined scarf, floating on the coastal waters of the Atlantic. Lights from the street, from the apartments and office buildings, flickered in the darkness, multiplied by their reflections off the glass of windows, storefronts, and shiny cars. Night was wrapped tightly around the city and its chill penetrated Gilda. She moved so quickly that she was invisible to anyone looking down from one of the windows of the towering apartment buildings of Riverside Drive. The rustle of leaves was the only sign that she passed through the night air. A pedestrian, out for an evening stroll by the river, might feel the brush of an unexpectedly warm breeze. But Gilda was a whirlwind of emotion as she sped downtown to the danger she knew was also hurtling through the night toward her home.

Gilda's thoughts were a kaleidoscopic blur. She glimpsed the calm and elegant face of Effie, her brow furrowed with concern, then an image of the home they shared in lower Manhattan, with its startling murals of foreign cities created by her dear brother Julius. The almond-shaped eyes of her tenant, Marci de Justo, who'd become almost as close a friend as those of her blood. Vivid sounds of Celia Cruz and Ismael Miranda wafting down from Marci's audio speakers out over her backyard garden like a warm mist. The faces of Sorel, Anthony, Julius, and Marci—the men in her life—floated through. Gilda often laughed at the image of the incongruous quartet. Her fear that a fifth, Samuel, was about to destroy all she held so precious swelled in her throat, almost choking off the air to her lungs. She pushed herself to move even faster.

Gilda easily recalled earlier threats Samuel had made. There had been many in the ninety years they'd known each other. They were usually accompanied by vengeful attacks, in the dark, from behind, under cover of innocence. But this time it had been a veiled hint, so subtle Gilda wondered if she were imagining the menace she felt when Samuel had spoken her name.

"The not-so-fair Gilda lives, I see," Samuel had said casually, as if he were simply observing the movements of a bug beneath his feet. His repeated use of the word *fair* reverberated now as a warning. Samuel continued to be the threat he'd always been.

In less time than it took to think Samuel's name, Gilda had traversed the four miles downtown and was standing outside the door of her garden apartment. Located in a renovated brick building she'd owned for thirty years, the rooms provided both the privacy Gilda required and a natural place in the neighborhood that nourished her as much as the blood that maintained her long life.

She listened and was startled to hear such quiet enveloping the building. Peering at the two tall windows that faced the street, and then through the intricate paintings Julius had applied to each pane, she saw the warm amber glow which bathed the front rooms. She unlocked the wrought-iron gate shielding her door and entered the spacious parlor.

As she'd come to spend more time with Gilda, Effie had added her own influences to the sparely decorated room. Fresh flowers sat on the low, cherry wood table in the center. A piece of Kente cloth was draped over the back of the overstuffed sofa, and a small painting by Julius now hung between the tall windows. Gilda looked around, satisfied that her home seemed the same as usual.

She drew in her breath and listened more closely. Around her she heard the muted noises of her tenants; directly above, it sounded as if Marci were enjoying a romantic evening. But in her own flat, she sensed no one. As she reached for the key to unlock the sleeping room her hands trembled with anxiety. *No one* could mean *no one alive*. She flung open the heavy metal door which was paneled to look like oak and was relieved when it crashed against the wall and revealed an uninhabited room. The thick silk of the oriental carpet glistened in soft light. The yellow satin comforter rested on the sleeping platform where the soil of Gilda's home state was mixed with that of others of her family. Her eyes burned with the memory of the ritual blending—dark earth sprinkled together and sewn into layered pallets that allowed any of her family to rest in this place in safety. The wave of emotions was for those whose earth blended here with hers and for the many whose did not.

Gilda closed and locked the door, puzzled. Earlier she'd been certain she'd sensed that Effie was in danger. Samuel's fearsome cruelty had shone in his eyes, brighter than sunlight, and Effie had seemed to be his focus. She opened the door to the garden, clinging to the hope that it, too, would be unchanged. She rushed out to the small patch of roses, rhododendron, and the queenly evergreen, turning in circles—relieved and frustrated. Danger was still near, Gilda knew it with all the molecules of her blood, but where?

She looked up at Marci's open windows. The shades were pulled down. A pale red glow emanated from inside, where music played softly. The red light was a sign that Marci was entertaining. Gilda watched the shadows on the window for a minute listening, but despite the music the room was cloaked in intimacy. Then Marci appeared at the window, snapping the shade up and lifting the window.

"*Hermana,* what are you doing down there? Is there something?" Marci leaned low out of the window, his shoulders swathed in a pale yellow silk blouse.

"I was just wondering where Effie might be." Gilda held her voice steady, letting it float on the air, falsely casual.

"Sister, she don't come up here with no red light, you know that." Marci laughed, as the picture tickled him. "She was there. Then she went out, downtown, I think."

Gilda marveled at how Marci could tell which direction people walked when they left the building, even though his apartment faced the back. He had a preternatural connection with all the tenants, listening to them, their needs, their troubles. The mother hen of the building, he offered his vibrant wisdom spun from the practical Puerto Rican reality of his childhood and grounded in the ancient Taino spirits. It amazed Gilda how each of the tenants accommodated their own reluctant reliance on a Puerto Rican drag queen who'd made them his family when his own had rejected him. As the men around him succumbed in greater numbers to the unnamed disease, Marci traveled across town, to the Bronx or Queens, to help out bar acquaintances and old friends indiscriminately. He dispensed *mafongo* and advice liberally to everyone, as if his thick stew and experiences were a universal resource.

In the years since she'd acquired the building, Marci had become her guide to the mortal world around their home. His music, the smell of his food, the love he showed for her and their building had made it a place of easy rest.

"Gotta go." Marci's voice sparkled in the night air.

"Hey, I thought you were single as of last month?"

"Not tonight."

"Marci...are you being careful?"

He looked down at Gilda, affecting the face of a wounded child.

"Manuel de Justo," Gilda said solemnly. She knew how much he hated anyone to use his given name. "*Ten cuidado!*"

"Of course, I am the soul of careful." Marci's long lashes lowered modestly as his lips curled in a brilliant smile and he withdrew inside.

What a strange existence, Gilda thought. She warned her friend to be cautious of blood that had become dangerous in this decade. Young men were sickening and dying so quickly that Gilda was uncertain how severely even she might be weakened by the infection. But her heightened senses enabled her to easily detect any illness and sidestep its perils. She'd helped tend to many and still the affliction, just like her own nature, remained a mystery to her. She looked up at the window; there was no further movement in the ruby light. Quiet blanketed the building and Gilda felt afraid again.

She returned to her living room, beginning to trace the energy of Effie's route in the air, then noticed the slip of paper sticking out from beneath the vase of yellow roses: *Sorel and Anthony are back. Cocktails. E.*

Excitement flooded Gilda, pushing thoughts of Samuel from her mind. Sorel and Anthony, who'd helped her learn her way through the world of their kind, were her blood family, bound to her as surely as her mother who'd died in slavery on a Mississippi plantation. Effie, who was newer in Gilda's life, was also part of this family, now linked with dozens of others around the world. As she closed up her house and again raced through New York's city streets, Gilda's fear mixed with anticipation. It was only when she stood on the corner of the lower Manhattan street where Sorel and Anthony maintained their establishment that she slowed enough to savor the feel of cobblestones beneath her feet. She could sense the three of them inside together, safe.

It had been almost a decade since Sorel and Anthony had made the difficult journey across the Atlantic to visit old friends and places they'd not seen for over a century. The moments Gilda spent apart from her family always seemed to fly by, yet they weighed on her heavily. She had not learned how to let the years pass and trust in the future. In that way she felt too much like Samuel, who also clung to the past. His rage at Gilda from almost a century before was as fresh for him as a new wound. The woman who'd betrayed him for Gilda had been dead longer now than she'd been alive. Gilda pushed the memory away from her, just as she wished she could do with Samuel.

The door of Sorel and Anthony's small bar was set right on the street, the ground level of an ancient factory which they owned. On the outside the door was covered by a modest sheet of metal, like many lining the block. The seventeenth-century carved wood from Spain attached to the interior side of the door made it hang heavily in the frame. Once inside, Gilda leaned back on the intricate, hard forms which pressed into her back as she breathed deeply.

Sorel, in evening wear accentuated by a gold embroidered vest, sat in his booth holding Effie's hand. The bar was appointed like an elegant pub: wood paneling, coats of arms, gleaming crystal. It had deeply padded stools with backs, two of which were now occupied by people familiar to Gilda. The four booths, other than Sorel's, were empty.

Anthony, wearing a blue silk suit rather than his usual apron, poured the wine expertly. Champagne for Sorel, a deep red for Effie. Gilda nodded a greeting at the thin, dark man behind the bar who'd worked with Anthony and Sorel since they'd opened the establishment long ago. He proffered her a champagne flute in a fluid movement. Gilda didn't break her stride as she took the glass and continued toward the dark green leather upholstered booth at the back.

"Ah, at last." Sorel rose from his seat, his rotund body moving lithely. His pale, delicate fingers encircled her large brown hand. "My daughter. I've missed you like sweet air."

Gilda never knew how to bridge these chasms. So much time seemed like only moments, yet their emotions were full. If tears had been possible for them, their eyes would have been brimming. Instead they squeezed each other's hands, letting the magnitude of their happiness pulse between them.

When Gilda sat next to Effie her body completely relaxed. She looked up into Anthony's sardonic gaze.

"So you are still drinking this poor excuse for wine?" he asked, nodding at the champagne flute.

"Anthony, you know I take after Sorel in that regard. The champagne grape has captured my soul almost as assuredly as Effie."

"Effie, at least, does not leave the blood sluggish."

"Thank you, Anthony." Effie's light voice carried a music of its own, distilled from hundreds of years of travel. She sipped the red wine through smiling lips. Gilda brushed her finger across Effie's mouth, enjoying the warm fullness, savoring her relief at seeing her beloved safe. As their skin touched, Gilda sensed, not for the first time, Effie holding something hidden inside herself. She pushed the sensation away and enjoyed her relief.

Sorel observed Gilda recognize a secret place inside Effie and wondered how they would weather the coming years. He and Anthony had spent almost two centuries of living together, striking a balance between the separations they both appreciated and their desire to experience life side by side. The separations—sometimes weeks, sometimes years—were part of the growing process for them. Living on one's own developed survival skills, helping each one of their family stay connected to the world and not withdraw into self-contained enclaves. It was within those isolated clans that the deadly patronizing attitude toward mortals was cultivated. Those, like Samuel, who took no responsibility for their existence thrived within the hidden enclaves. Each decade he grew thick with paranoia and the blood of terrified victims slaughtered like deer in season.

Sorel understood how difficult the separations were for Gilda. As he held her hand he could feel both her joy at his return and the edge of anxiety that anticipated his next trip. More than a hundred years had passed since Gilda's enslavement and the death of her mother under its brutality, yet she could still barely withstand separations. Every journey away from her felt like a move toward abandonment. Overcoming this fear was a lesson Sorel was confident Gilda would learn in time. As he'd sat with Effie, he sensed her compelling need to move back out into the world. The lesson would be brought home to Gilda soon.

"We have so much to tell you about the land we left behind. It has changed, as you can imagine."

Laughter burst from Gilda and Effie, knowing that the last time Anthony and Sorel had seen France, Marie Antoinette was about to be led to the guillotine.

"But you have things to discuss with us, I believe." Sorel took a sip from his glass then sat back in the booth. Effie turned to Gilda, seeing the thoughts behind her eyes for the first time. Effie was small in the booth beside Sorel, her blue-black skin glistening in the soft light that bathed the room.

"What is it?" Effie's voice was low and steady, even as the muscles in her body became alert. Her tiny figure coiled tightly with energy as she took in Gilda's concern.

"I don't want to spoil your homecoming," Gilda said, looking up at Anthony. She could feel him probing her mind, not waiting for her to speak.

"Samuel." Anthony spit the name out.

"Yes."

"Samuel? I'd hoped we were done with him," Effie said, her voice as hard and sharp as a steel dagger.

"He came to me tonight. On the street. Again. Full of syrup overlaying the vinegar."

Anthony drank from his glass, placed it firmly on the table, and walked away. The set of his back told them how angry he was.

"Did he make threats again?" Effie asked.

"Not directly. He said something about seeing in the turn of the century together, as we had in the past."

"He is a bit early," Sorel said, trying to mask his anxiety. "Off-schedule as is his usual."

"But he made several references that worried me. He kept using the word fair in odd ways. Not so odd really, just repeatedly. I didn't think anything of it at first. Then he disappeared with such a sense of bemusement I was…" Gilda stopped, unsure what to say. She looked to Effie, whose brow was wrinkled in thought; then at Sorel, who looked alarmed. He'd known Samuel longer than any of them and understood that Gilda's concern was not misplaced.

"Why does he continue this? Eleanor has been dead for almost one hundred years!" Effie spoke aloud before she thought.

Sadness passed over Sorel's face like a carnival mask. In her mortal life, Eleanor had been like a daughter to him, the sunny face of curiosity and hopefulness all of them struggled to hold on to. Her spirit was as golden as the hills of Yerba Buena, where miners dug for precious ore.

"He's always blamed Gilda. Even Eleanor's death can't release him." Sorel's voice deepened with sorrow. Everyone was silent as he closed his eyes. His beautiful hands rested lightly on the table as the image of Eleanor sprang to life in his mind. The way she tossed her auburn hair had remained unchanged from the time she was five until the day she died—haughty and vulnerable at the same time. Sorel could almost feel the brush of it against his hand. But the picture he examined behind his eyes also revealed the glint of petulance in hers. Many of their blood acted deliberately cruel or brutal, and Eleanor had done both. Yet there'd been no meanness in her. She'd cared deeply about everything, in the moment. Samuel and Gilda had both entranced her. But her most enduring care was for herself and her whims.

He'd brought Eleanor into their family impulsively. She had

repeated that same mistake with Samuel, then abandoned him in pursuit of others. It didn't matter to Samuel that Gilda was only one of many lovers she preferred to him.

Sorel opened his eyes, no longer able to bear the shining clarity of his memory. "I'll call him to me, make him see some sense."

"Sorel, this isn't your responsibility," Gilda said. She, too, remembered the feel of Eleanor, as well as all she might have done to keep Eleanor by her side. But she'd refused to accommodate Eleanor's profoundest desire—Samuel's death. "He was Eleanor's error in judgment, not yours."

"If we follow lineage, he is my mistake too."

"Don't blame yourself." Effie spoke from many more years of experience than even Sorel. "At some point, troublesome people have to take responsibility for their own actions."

"Samuel is not someone we can assume will recognize good sense, even if it's pointed out to him," Gilda said. "This time there'll be no avoiding him."

"I'm afraid you're wholly correct, Gilda." Anthony had returned to the table carrying a small wood box. Gilda was startled by the way the hardness in Anthony's voice mirrored Effie's. It was as if they knew a secret no one else could comprehend and they meant her to follow their lead without thought or sentiment.

The box sat ominously on the table. It was rough-hewn but had three finely made bronze clasps. Anthony sat down beside Sorel, whose usually jovial expression was unreadable.

Gilda stared at the box, unwilling to focus on what lay inside it.

"I think we can manage Samuel," Effie said.

"I'm sure you can," Anthony said, "but with this you both can avoid undue—"

"Please stop talking as if Samuel were a cockroach I'm going to squash under my boot. That's just how Samuel thinks!" Gilda's voice rose with emotion. "We spend so much of our time learning to respect life, to live beside mortals and share the world in a responsible way. Don't talk about disposing of Samuel as if he'd never been human, or one of us."

"Samuel listens to no one," Effie said, her anger tightening her throat. She pushed her glass away from her and locked Gilda in her gaze. "Everywhere we turn there are the angry ones, full of rage with no idea how they got that way. They have some vague idea of injustice and a hunger for redress. And nothing else."

"Not all of us can cast off our sorrow easily," Sorel said.

"Samuel's life is a poison to all of us, whatever his sorrows. And we are the ones who hold the responsibility for him, no one else," Effie continued. She finally looked away toward Anthony. "All of you know his hatred for Gilda."

They were silent in their assent. She went on, unable to let her feelings remain unspoken. "If it means not having to weep dry tears while I scatter the ashes of any of you…I will incinerate Samuel."

Effie's anger was a wave of icy air in the room. Gilda had never seen her so implacable.

"But how can we say he's irredeemable? Eleanor may have made a poor decision, but we can't compound it." Gilda's voice was tight with pleading. "She cared enough to bring him into our family. We have to give him some chance."

They could feel the others in the room straining not to appear to hear their conversation, but the words would be as clear to the other patrons and the bartender as if whispered next to their ears. The clink of ice in glasses and the movement of the air around the room punctuated the rising emotion.

"Samuel was a choice she regretted almost immediately," Anthony stated. "He's tried to harm you more than once. Don't sentimentalize."

Gilda inhaled deeply, not willing to embrace the idea of destruction. "Tonight coming home, I encountered a young black man much like Samuel. Bitter, disappointed. He assumed by attacking me, maybe raping me, he'd make himself a man. Have something to share with his brothers." Gilda hurried as she felt them resist her story. "I know many men who look at women like they watch sports. I'm not sentimentalizing anything. When he touched me I could have killed him, tossed his body in the river, and few would have noticed his absence. But inside him was a boy who'd been hurt. When I was able to find that clear space I could help him. I know we can't always help. But when do we stop trying?"

It was at these moments that Sorel felt most weary and at the same time most proud. "If you want to handle Samuel on your own," he spoke softly, "I won't interfere. Not yet." He pushed the box across the table back toward Anthony. "But I assure you neither Anthony nor I will hesitate to protect you."

Gilda sat back in the booth and said, "Let's not talk about this any more then. I think Samuel is simply succeeding in making us give him attention while he's sitting somewhere laughing with that horrible braying he has."

Gilda didn't believe the words even as she spoke them. Nor did her companions, but they let the conversation turn to Sorel and Anthony's trip to Europe. The anxiety remained at the table, seated silently with them.

Effie and Gilda walked northward toward home slowly, enjoying the sporadic lights of lower Broadway and the people who moved around them. As they got closer to Chelsea, Gilda felt her muscles tense, anticipating the danger awaiting her. She saw that Effie, too, was listening with her body.

"I don't think I've ever known such fear. Not since I escaped the plantation as a child," Gilda said almost in a whisper.

"Yes. There is something about being hunted silently that never leaves the blood."

"I can't deliberately kill him. I made the choice to let go of my mortality, but not humanity."

"I understand that, Gilda. But you need to understand Samuel has given away his humanity."

"I don't believe that."

"Then why did you rush home in terror?"

Gilda's hand went automatically to her throat, but she could not answer Effie. She still felt him clawing at her and could, if she let herself, still sense the murderous lust pouring through his hands as he tried to rip her life from her. Yet Gilda clung to the possibility of his goodness as desperately as he'd gripped her throat.

"He let go finally, and so must you," Effie said, expressing no regret for listening to Gilda's thoughts. The remaining blocks to their home were traversed in silence, neither Effie nor Gilda speaking or thinking.

The glow of their windows felt like a lighthouse, guiding them to a comfortable berth after storm-tossed open seas. Once inside they shed their clothes and with them the scent of fear. As always, they both listened to the building, assuring themselves that each of the tenants was safe. The apartments were wrapped in sleep except for Marci's, where the stereo still played softly over the energy of desire.

"He must be in love!" Gilda said with laughter.

"This is news." Effie unlocked the door to the sleeping room and pulled the comforter back. The soft sheen of the black satin sheet covering their pallets was inviting in the light of the candle Effie lit.

"He was wearing that yellow blouse that looks so beautiful on his skin when I saw him earlier this evening." Gilda followed her. "And grinning like a Halloween mask."

"That sounds like love," Effie said, and reached out to pull Gilda down to her.

"Your affection for Eleanor, your feelings of guilt for not staying with her, has made Samuel a cause you cannot win. I don't want to leave here worried that you'll end your life in a foolish battle with him."

Gilda stiffened in Effie's arms, but Effie held on to her. The truth of the moment raced between them like an electrical current. Gilda had known even without the words. Sorel and Anthony spent most of their days and nights together. But often they separated for months, and sometimes years. Bird, who'd helped bring Gilda into this life, who'd known her even before they did, had traveled unceasingly, stopping only occasionally to look into her daughter Gilda's face. Each of them had told her this was their way to maintain the sense of anticipation and wonder at life. To keep returning to the world alone, seeking to learn from mortals. Alone gave them a connection they'd never get keeping themselves apart. But Gilda still didn't know how to manage the long days when she had no one to lie with.

The natural pattern of eternal life frightened Gilda, it felt too much like an abyss. When she was a child she'd watched the overseer carrying her mother's body from their room. She understood it was no longer her mother, but now simply a "thing," just as the slave master had always insisted. At that moment she'd been consumed by knowing she'd never see her birth mother again. A huge vacuum had opened in front of her, sucking her into a breathless, infinite hole, an abyss she'd spent her subsequent years running from.

"It is our rhythm of living, my love. We are always together, even when we part. You've seen that with Bird, Anthony, Sorel. Good heavens, even with Samuel!" The sinewy muscle of Effie's arm held tight. The years Effie had spent wandering the world far outnumbered those of Anthony and Sorel. She enjoyed the many lives she'd touched as time passed and knew that Gilda would never be at ease until she, too, fully accepted the change in perspective that was necessary to their kind.

Gilda rested her head in the soft part of Effie's neck at her shoulder. She couldn't deny what was true: when she'd raced home in fear for Effie's safety, she'd already known that the time was near for Effie to return to her travels.

"When?" Gilda asked.

"Let's not talk with our voices now," Effie said, covering Gilda's mouth with hers. At first Gilda could not respond. The ashes that would have been tears filled her mouth and eyes. Then the heat of Effie's lips drew her. Effie leaned backward onto the bed, her small breasts appealing in the dark. She pulled Gilda down to her. The moist earth shifted gently beneath them as Gilda let her weight press into Effie.

The desire they held for each other was heightened by their imminent separation, and for the first time, Gilda could let herself feel the anticipation of that moment when they'd see each other again.

Gilda stopped resisting, and her passion pinned Effie to their bed. She thrust down, feeling Effie's body meet hers. This was the first woman she'd ever made love to with the fullness of desire. She remembered so many fleeting touches, moments when desire floated around her like bright bubbles until she wiped them away into the air. Now she wanted to breathe them in as she did when drinking Sorel's beloved champagne. With Effie she'd learned to open, to meet the needs of her body that ran just as deep as blood.

Pushing her knee between Effie's legs, Gilda straddled her tight thigh muscle and set a rhythmic pace that kept time with their breathing. Each inhalation drove them deeper into their hunger for each other. When Gilda felt they were both ready she slipped inside Effie, gently letting the tide of their desire guide her. The muscles in Gilda's arm tightened to solid cords as her thrusts grew more insistent and Effie's embrace tightened. Their bodies pulsated on the firm pallet in a rhythm both old and new. The sound of their breathing and the wetness of Effie's body rocking on Gilda's hand filled the locked room. Everything around them was forgotten until Effie exploded into Gilda's hand. Gilda's body stiffened as she continued pushing harder. She thrust against Effie, feeling every texture of her skin and feeling nothing at all except the wave crashing inside her. She muffled her final scream in the pillow at Effie's head.

The room vibrated with the passion that they'd released into the air. A damp mist floated above them as they both lay still until their breathing steadied.

Effie touched the softness of Gilda's close-cut hair and was pleased to sense the change in Gilda's understanding. The worry had sat uneasily on her for weeks. She'd used all her energy to shield Gilda from the conflict she felt. Now she was able to open.

Gilda pulled the comforter up around them and they drifted into the rest that usually claimed all of them in the pre-dawn hours. After only moments of listening to Effie's breathing slow to almost nothing, Gilda, too, was no longer awake. Their room was steeped in darkness maintained by the painted windows and heavy drapes that hung in front of them. Their rest was not governed by a diurnal clock, but ebbed and flowed with their energy. While night was their natural milieu and daylight could drain their energy, no hours were unavailable to them.

Just before the sun pushed against the covered window, Gilda's eyes opened. She stared into the inky air, uncertain why she was suddenly alert at that moment. The house remained quiet all around her. Too quiet.

Gilda reached out for Effie, who pulled herself back from sleep.

"He's here," Gilda said in a low hiss.

Effie was awake and reaching for her clothes within the moment. They both stepped into pants and sweaters as they listened to the air around them.

"The music," Effie said as she realized she could still hear a soft guitar from Marci's apartment above them. Without speaking, Gilda and Effie bolted through the doors and out into the hall. They moved silently up the stairs, afraid of what they'd find. Samuel was there. Using his powers he'd shrouded Marci's room so nothing could be perceived except the record on the stereo. They stood outside the door for only a second, then Effie twisted the knob off silently, the brass wrinkling between her fingers like paper before she dropped it to the floor. Gilda pushed the door open to Marci's living room. It glowed in red.

At first Gilda thought the walls were awash in blood, but then she realized it was the lamplight that usually shone down into their yard. The shade moved against the open window where a figure stood. Samuel stepped forward, his face twisted in hatred. The torn yellow silk of Marci's blouse lay at his feet. Gilda looked quickly around the room. On the far side, across the plush couch he'd been so proud of, Marci lay sprawled, blood still draining onto the floor from his wound.

Gilda ran to Marci and knelt on the floor. Around his head, blood had soaked into the cushions of the couch and then pooled on the floor beside him. His eyes fluttered behind his lids. Gilda's anger rose through her throat.

"You didn't even take his blood. You spilled it like sewage!" Gilda pressed her hand to the wound in Marci's neck, hoping to stem the flow before it was too late.

Effie took a step closer and looked over at Marci, saying, "I don't know, Gilda."

"Forget about him," said Samuel, the satisfaction clear in his voice.

"You were here with him, weren't you? When I was in the yard?"

Samuel's laughter was not mirthful. "Of course. The little slut was wiggling with glee. I could have slaughtered him right then, but I wanted you to see."

"No, Samuel. I think you wanted to be punished," Effie said, her voice unnaturally even.

Samuel was startled. He tried to move but found his limbs were sluggish.

"Marci de Justo! That's who you meant when you said 'fair.'" Gilda spoke her realization aloud as if it might reel the hours back in and she could save her friend.

"My fight is with Gilda." Samuel almost shouted at Effie.

"And what is that quarrel?"

"She knows."

"An unarticulated complaint is an answer withheld. Speak!"

"Gilda knows."

"An answer withheld is an embrace of ignorance."

Samuel's face was filled with as much puzzlement as fear each time Effie spoke.

"He's barely breathing!" Gilda said urgently, clenching her hand tightly around Marci's neck.

"Careful," Effie responded. "Press your lips to it."

"No! This isn't Marci's choice, I…"

"Do it. Gently let your fluids mix, but take nothing from him. Listen inside."

Samuel watched Gilda bend toward the small body. He doubted Marci could be revived without an infusion of blood and he believed Gilda too timid to give Marci life that way. He smirked in satisfaction that finally he'd found his revenge.

"Ignorance is a dull knife." Effie moved closer to Samuel, her muscles rippling like electricity under her clothes. Samuel thought he heard a noise in the yard below, but was afraid to turn his eyes from Effie.

"All I wanted was peace," he said, his voice a narrow whine that grated in the air.

"You wanted Eleanor to love you. She didn't! Can't you understand that? She didn't love anyone but herself," Effie said. She could feel Gilda's energy flowing through the room and sense Marci regaining consciousness. "Pull back!" she shouted.

Gilda raised her head and wiped Marci's blood from her mouth. The tiny portion of her blood she'd shared would give him the strength he needed without drawing him into their family against his wishes. She stood, placing Marci tenderly back onto the couch with his legs raised on pillows. "*Mi hermano,*" she murmured to him softly to quiet the terror which returned with his consciousness. The wound had closed, and she could feel fresh blood, enlivened by hers, coursing through his veins. His skin took on a more natural color as he struggled to open his eyes. Gilda rested her hands on his forehead, willing him into sleep.

"She wouldn't leave us in peace," Samuel said to Effie. It was somehow meant to explain the person bleeding on the couch.

"Peace is most difficult to endure, one of my teachers was fond of saying." Effie spoke as she moved closer to Samuel. His eyes hardened; he was unable to understand why he couldn't move. Effie held him in her gaze, not letting her anger or disgust distract her.

"You will now have peace," she said, clasping her two hands together as if to pray. Her swing curved smoothly up through the air, her blow knocking Samuel back against the window frame and cracking the wood. She hit him again as he bounced forward, and the glass shattered. He struggled back toward Effie.

"No!" Gilda said, her voice rising out of the deep place she'd always run from. The thick, guttural tone was like broken ice showering around them. Gilda's stride carried her across the room before either Effie or Samuel saw her move. Samuel reached out with both hands for her throat, as if he could silence her voice. Gilda dropped to her knees, eluding his grasp, and yanked Marci's ruined blouse from beneath Samuel's feet. The tear of the cloth reverberated in the room. With the shredded material gripped between her clenched fists, Gilda rose, swinging upward. Her blow caught Samuel under his chin, and she could hear his teeth clamp shut through his tongue. This time he fell back through the window as the shade snapped open.

Samuel still smiled during the few seconds of his fall, the blood of his severed tongue creasing his face. He was certain he could not be hurt by a two-story fall onto a garden. He'd survived much worse in his years.

At that moment, Anthony took a step away from the artfully carved box on the ground, moved off the carefully laid flagstones and into the path of Samuel's descent. He raised a broad silver dagger. His pale skin glistened in the darkness of the yard. The shining metal and colorful gems which adorned the handle caught the hint of morning light peeking over the horizon. The muscles of Anthony's arm were taut as he held the silver dagger before him. He admired its beauty just as Samuel's spine made contact with the tip. Anthony released his hold as Samuel's body swallowed the blade and crashed to the ground. He lay on the grass, the hilt of the sword driven into the ground, the bloody blade gleaming from his chest. Samuel's eyes opened in disbelief, then were empty.

Anthony looked up at the windows that surrounded the yard. All were dark and unoccupied except for Marci's, where Gilda and Effie looked down at him. "You will have peace now," he said. He pulled an edge of Samuel's coat up to protect his own hand as he gripped the blade of the knife and wrenched it downward, opening Samuel's chest. He then pushed the hilt deeper into the ground. Blood flowed like a stream into the roots of the evergreen. Anthony ripped at Samuel's clothes, removing the garments and shoes that held his protective soil. He then stepped back into the shadow of Gilda's garden door and watched morning break over the city.

Gilda and Effie locked Marci's door, leaving him enclosed in sleep until they woke him. When they stood beside Anthony at the garden door they clasped their friend's hands, slick with blood.

"His life was much too long, Gilda. He didn't have the spirit for it," Effie said.

"I'm sorry it ended here." Anthony spoke softly.

"We saved Marci. That's a balance, I think," Gilda answered.

"More than a balance," Effie added.

"Do you remember Joe Louis?" Gilda asked Effie.

"Of course. His power was amazing!"

"He'd have loved your swing," Gilda laughed.

"I think you might make the college team yourself," Effie said.

The three retreated into the house as the sun took over the sky. Before anyone else was awake to peer out their windows, it had turned Samuel's body into ash. Only the dagger was left in the soil. From above, its silver gleam looked like the tilted arm of a sundial greeting the day. Although the windows were painted and the curtains were already drawn, Effie tugged at their hems as if to fasten them more tightly.

"Come," Gilda said as she removed her clothes. After washing off the blood of their enemy and of their friend, they climbed into the wide bed. Effie, Gilda, and Anthony pulled the gold comforter up and turned to fit into the curves of their bodies. Each left the other to personal thoughts.

Anthony remembered a time over a hundred years earlier when he'd helped the young Gilda wash away the filth of the road in a deep copper tub. At this cleansing tonight, he saw that naiveté was no longer a veil between her and the real world.

Effie's mind drifted over the roads she might follow now that Gilda had her own path.

Gilda was at first startled that Samuel's death was a relief more than a burden. She'd watched the muscles of his face soften and his eyes lose their hardness, finally understanding he'd locked himself inside a torment that had only this release. She fell into sleep planning to clean Marci's rooms before awakening him, wondering where she'd find him a new silk blouse.

They were all at rest before the sun's rays tapped at the shuttered windows.

APOSTATE PRINCESS

JUDITH KATZ

How lucky was I to find myself in New York City in America at the start of a new century! Horseless buggies ran through the middle of the street, and trains traveled underground. Jewish men walked about not only with their heads held high, but sometimes with their heads not even covered. Jewish women wore their own hair loose and wild, or piled up on top of their heads—but truly, their *own* hair. As if to prove that these liberties for women were not an illusion, Emma Goldman and other women, Jewish and gentile, stood in lecture halls advocating free love, anarchy, and a woman's right to vote. I should have blessed that execrable Princess Eugenia Vanstazia for sending me reeling off to such a place. And yet, I damned her.

Even here in paradisical America, where I was free to walk the streets without fear of being spat at, I am sorry to tell you that I missed that accursed princess every day of my new life, from the moment I awoke in the morning until I fell to sleep at night. She was in me like a prayer; she filled me as the words of God filled the pious. It was ridiculous,

I know, given the circumstances—we had kept each other's company less than half a year, and I had known the sweetness of her kisses only that one unforgettable Shabbes eve. In all the time of her long absence I heard from her just as I prepared to depart from Poland, one hastily delivered cable which came to me as I made my way to the train. And it's a good thing, too, that I did not delay my departure from Cracow in order to read her message, which in the end, proved stingy and self serving. Oh, it began with promise—MY DEAR ANNA DAVIDOVICH, SHALOM, SHALOM—although any moron not lovesick as I was would have read that "dear" as a sign of politeness, not a blandishment of love. I should have seen it right away, the *"shalom"* was meant in the broadest sense of the word—hello and good-bye. And what else did she say in her short missive? Only this: SACRED PRAYER BOOK LOST (STOP) MUST RETRIEVE IT AT ONCE (STOP) IF YOU FIND IT PLEASE SEND TO PLOVDIV (STOP), after which followed a Bulgarian address which proved to be as long as the message itself. Finally she ended: ALL BEST WISHES (STOP) I REMAIN PRINCESS EUGENIA VANSTAZIA (STOP) YOUR FRIEND.

Any sane person would have taken that meager note, torn it to shreds, and let it fly out the window across the Polish countryside, and right behind it that accursed prayer book, which as you recall the princess left on my nightstand that one night we kissed and drove each other wild. Of course I had it with me now in my new life. I had taken her absent-minded leaving of that prayer book as a love gift, a token of her passion. But there on the train I flung away neither the princess' prayer book nor her terse cable. I kept that yellow paper with its taped-on words, and as the train shot across the countryside all the way from Cracow to Gdansk, I composed various replies to the princess in my head. I considered whether to send her prayer book back to her, or whether to tell her she must come to America, find me at my brother's house, and fetch it herself. I thought to act as if I'd never received her cable at all.

But soon after I boarded the steamer that would take me to New York, as the fine ship pulled out of Gdansk harbor and I stood on the deck and watched the coast of a country I would never return to slip further and further away, I knew what I must do. When the shores of Poland were no more than a thin sliver on the eastern horizon, I went down to my cabin and composed a note to the princess. *I have not your prayer book in my possessions,* I told her. *I am bound for America. Perhaps some day I will see you there. I remain yours, faithfully, Anna Davidovich.* Of course I lied to her, how could I not? That little book remained in my carpetbag with my other lovers' treasures. It was all I had left of my greatest, most sorrowful love.

I sealed my note to Princess Eugenia Vanstazia, addressed it, and placed it with her cable between the pages of the prayer book in question, then returned the whole package to my bag. The rest of the long journey proved uneventful. The sea was calm for most of our trip, and I passed my time reading poetry and novels by American authors, so as to improve my English. The food in my class was lavish, but little appealed to me. The sea was gray, my heart was heavy. In fourteen days' time we reached Ellis Island.

I was dazed from my journey and a bit off balance, what with all the commotion and noise we immigrants made as we arrived in New York. Yet I passed my short inquisition at the hands of the customs men with flying colors, and after producing identification papers, certificates of birth, and a letter in English from my brother Stephan which explained his relation to me, I was allowed to pass into America with relatively little humiliation. Stephan himself was waiting for me with open arms. I was exhausted and so saw only that he was well dressed and seemed cheerful. In all the commotion I never saw how drawn he looked, how America had changed him from a relaxed playboy into a harder playing man.

We took the ferry to Manhattan, then Stephan hailed a *droshky.* We had a long ride up the east side of Manhattan, past Jewish and other immigrant vendors, past carts full of flowers and men who walked quickly beside one another, all the way to Central Park, where Stephan kept a huge apartment. He didn't live down with our Polish *lantsmen,* among the garment workers and shopkeepers, but up here, with the German Jews, who had established themselves in a place far enough from the hustle and bustle of the old country that they could forget it, and close enough that in a half hour's time they could ride in a coach or a taxicab down to Orchard Street and be reminded of the taste of a good pickle or a marvelous knish as clearly as day.

Stephan paid the *droshky* driver to carry my bags up to our apartment. He tipped the man handsomely. Then, with a great display of charm and elegance, Stephan took my arm and gave me a tour of my new home. In the foyer was a photograph of our parents, arm in arm, as if they too were welcoming me to my new life. We went down a long hallway, and Stephan waved his arm like a magician. "Here is the parlor, dear sister, and here," he gave another grand sweep, "the dining room." With great ceremony he drew back a pair of heavy wooden doors to reveal a magnificent library full of handsome bookshelves and a small writing desk. "This room is yours to use as you desire." He showed me his bedroom, which was dark but not unpleasant. Next, with an arm around my waist, he guided me across the hall to a bright, lovely bedroom with chintz curtains, a dressing table, and a beautiful chest of drawers.

"Your room, my sister," offered Stephan with a slight bow.

"Oh, Stephan, it's a lovely room."

That room would have been half a house in certain parts of Cracow. Indeed, later when new friends took me to see the tenements in which so many of our people lived on the lower east side of New York, I realized that my bedroom alone could have slept a family of four *and* a boarder. "It's all mine?"

"All yours." He looked at me gravely. "But look, you are thin. Come, I must feed you. I hope you are hungry."

Now that I was finally here in America I was famished. With a wink, Stephan led me back through the apartment to a kitchen even bigger than my bedroom. The floor was covered with black-and-white tiles, the counters were made of metal, and painted white. There were cabinets for storage, an icebox practically as big as the piano, and a stove so white and gleaming it almost made me weep. Stephan opened the icebox and presented me with a lunch of cold chicken and *challa,* then poured himself a glass of vodka. He smacked his lips. "This is illegal in America. To even own a bottle of vodka is against the law." He winked at me. "But I have friends—"

"What kind of friends?" I asked.

"Finish your lunch, Annushka, then you must rest. For tonight we have a little party and you'll meet them all."

"My first night in New York? I barely speak their language."

Stephan poured himself another glass of vodka and held it up to me in a kind of toast. "These friends all speak Yiddish in one form or another. They're a little rough around the edges but they love a good party. I can think of no better way to welcome you home."

It turned out these little parties were my brother Stephan's main business in life, that and traveling even further uptown to Harlem, where he frequented nightclubs and gambling parlors. It is to all of our good fortune that he was a decent gambler and could always stay at least one step ahead of the dealer. It is to my particular good fortune that I kept my share of our inheritance separate from his and had none of his taste for betting on cards or horses. Stephan lived solely off his inheritance and money he brought home from these long card games. Here I was expecting to be introduced into high Jewish society, and who were his best friends? A pack of well-dressed men of dubious character from Budapest and Belgrade, Bucharest and Prague. One of these fellows even hailed from Uruguay by way of Moscow. To tell you the truth, I did not like any of them much, for they smoked and they drank, and when they brought women along, they were always too young and too pretty and very foolish.

So it became my habit when my brother had his little gatherings that I would go off to a lecture, of which there were a great many in those days. It was on occasions such as these, while my brother was drinking his contraband liquor and smoking cigars, that I, in fact, heard Emma Goldman speak, and also Dr. Sigmund Freud, and even once, the inventor of the automobile. Indeed, it was after one such evening that I learned more about my lost Princess Eugenia Vanstazia than I wished ever to know.

To be sure, as each day I became more and more accustomed to life in America, I also spent a good part of that day hoping against hope that some business venture, some royal duty, or yes, even some new love, would bring that troublesome princess to New York. I imagined myself strolling with my brother under a parasol in Central Park, and there she would be, on the arm of a man much younger than she, or perhaps alone, under her own parasol, walking a small dog. I would still my heart and remind myself that such an eventuality was possible but unlikely. That if the princess were to resurface in my life, she would do it as she had the first time and catch me completely unawares.

But my news of the princess when it came came secondhand, and for this, strange as it sounds, I am grateful.

It was a lovely spring evening, some months after my arrival in New York. Stephan informed me that he was having one of his parties that evening, and I could be sure that the apartment would be lively with cigar smoke. I had, by that time, investigated certain financial possibilities to keep me secure and also out of harm's way should Stephan's extravagances cause his good fortune to reverse itself. I had opened a little tea shop not far from where we lived on the edges of Central Park. Unlike the shop I kept in Poland, this one was open only from seven in the morning until three in the afternoon. I employed one young woman to bake and one to serve, as I had done in Cracow, and to my delight I could run a business and keep myself afloat with half the effort it took back home.

Just that afternoon an extraordinarily handsome woman who spoke with a strong German accent came into the tea shop for lunch. She was accompanied by another woman who looked ragged by comparison, though to be truthful, both women seemed to have been through much in their lives and were quite beautiful. The German woman introduced herself as Bertha Pappenheim and told me that she would be speaking that evening in the West Village on the difficult topic of white slavery. Her associate, who was introduced as Sara Koblentz, handed me a broadside on which was printed all the pertinent information. I had heard of white slavery in Cracow. It was a horrifying practice whereby men, even Jewish men, would trick young women into marriage, then steal them away from their homes and employ them as prostitutes. Of course, when I heard those stories I never believed they could be true.

"Trust me, madame, they are too true. Please, attend my lecture this evening and you will learn the terrible facts." Miss Pappenheim handed me a half dollar, and with her associate, bowed slightly and left.

Since my brother had evening plans, and I had not yet settled on my own, I took this meeting as good fortune. I was more than a little interested in Miss Pappenheim's subject, and to be frank, I was intrigued by both her and her mysterious assistant. So at seven o'clock, just as my brother's roguish friends began to arrive, I made my way down to the west village to hear the lady speak.

As was often the case at these talks, the audience was full of women and men, most concerned with the topic at hand, but some who questioned the authority of the lecturer. At such point as a man in a tweed suit with a gold watch chain began shouting his incredulity from the audience, Miss Pappenheim invited her associate, the very woman I had seen with her in my shop, to join her on the podium. There on the stage I saw that although Sara Koblentz was incredibly weary, she was most attractive. She looked older than Miss Pappenheim; she seemed older even than I. And there was a quality about her, a kind of hardness around her shoulders and eyes, that made me wonder what great sorrow she had lived through or seen. I did not wait long to find out, for Sara told her story and it was horrifying. As a young girl she had been tricked into the evil trade by a brother and sister who stole her from Warsaw and brought her to Argentina. Over time she was made to not only perform the most depraved acts for customers of the bordello (there were audible gasps from the audience) but was also forced to engage in various charades to help kidnap other women like herself. Such a life led her to partake of opium and hashish, but soon even these could not soothe her, and eventually she found herself traveling the world with nothing more or less than murder in her heart.

"Finally, through bad fortune and good, I found my way to Miss Pappenheim, who has taken me with her to lecture, to tell you all that I know."

First there was awed silence, but soon the audience burst into applause and before long we were all on our feet. Not since I heard Emma Goldman speak on the pleasures and necessities of free love had I felt such passion and power from a speaker. Clearly this woman had undergone some kind of miraculous transformation. How I wished Princess Vanstazia could be with me to witness this, for it was far more powerful than any religious experience. This woman had changed her own life even at the furthest distance from God.

As the crowd dispersed, I made my way to the front of the hall. I extended my hand to both speakers and was surprised and delighted when Sara Koblentz took my hand with both of her own.

"What a remarkable story. How miraculous that you are alive to tell it!"

To my great surprise, Sara Koblentz blushed. "I am honored that you came to hear it."

"Perhaps you can join me for tea this evening."

"I've a few ends to tie up with Miss Pappenheim, and then I am free." With that she continued to shake hands, then had a few words with Miss Pappenheim, who was busy talking to a group of well-heeled men in suits.

"Analysts," said Sara. "They'll talk poor Bertha's ear off until dawn tomorrow."

"Analysts?" I asked.

"Why yes," said Sara Koblentz. "Miss Pappenheim, in her other life, is a patient of the world famous psychiatrist, Dr. Sigmund Freud."

Because the tea shops in the West Village were crowded and noisy, we struck upon the idea of hailing a taxi uptown and taking tea privately in my own little shop. I ushered us in the back way, lit a low light so as not to attract customers, and set the pot to boil. I arranged a few sweets on a china plate and set them before Miss Koblentz. When the tea was brewed, I brought it to our table and opened my hands.

"It is a small offering, but I don't dare bring you home where there is a larder full of substantial food. My brother keeps rough company—"

"Not rougher than I'm used to," answered Sara. "Who knows, I may know some of his friends by more than their names. I have survived viciousness at the hands of all manner of men and women, even women higher born than yourself."

I poured her tea but I was breathless. Here was a woman who might have been dead five times over, and yet she survived it all.

"And in the bargain, I have seen the world." Sara's eyes twinkled. "As it happens, through great coincidence, I might even know a special friend of yours by more than just her name."

I looked at this woman, dressed in fine clothes but with a map of every kind of suffering etched deeply around her mouth and eyes.

"But Miss Koblentz, you have seen the roughest side of the world. I have lived in relative gentility all my life. Who could we possibly know in common?"

"My dear Anna Davidovich," my new friend said, "think about your broken heart."

I looked at mysterious Sara across the table. Her face remained unreadable in the lamplight. My heart began to beat swiftly. How could such a woman as this, a woman who had been disabused by butchers and rabbis, know anything about my cloistered heart?

Sara Koblentz spoke after a long silence. "The wide gray ocean keeps us far from our sorrows, does it not, Anna Davidovich? And yet when the wind blows a certain way, the waves bear messages we never expect. I knew the minute I heard your name that we had one important acquaintance in common. In your case, she sent you running. In my case, she set me free."

Without thinking I brought one hand to my face and covered my breasts with the other, as if I were naked. "That's impossible! Do you have mystical powers as well as powers of great survival?"

"No, my dear." Sara pushed a wisp of faded red hair out of her eyes and let out a raspy laugh. "It is only that the Princess Eugenia Vanstazia has a loose and selfish tongue. And she believed you had something she left with you and wanted back."

Now I was completely off balance. My breath was gone. Still I managed to sputter out another question. "How could you know the princess? Why would she mention my name?"

Sara Koblentz put her hand out to me. She stroked my arm. "Dear Miss Davidovich, Princess Vanstazia and I were close in the same way you have been close. She never asked me to teach her a foreign language, though in our exchanges we did freely use our tongues."

I sat up now and considered, should I throw my new friend out of my shop into the city streets or should I hear her story? My jealous heart got the better of me, so I asked, "When did you see her last?"

Sara Koblentz pulled her chair close to my own. She slipped her arms around me. "It was some months ago. Not long, I believe, after she said good-bye to you."

"And she mentioned my name?"

"Many times." Sara took a sip of tea. "Listen carefully. I will tell you all I know.

"It was the winter in Poland and I had been wandering for quite some time. As you heard tonight, my life had taken a series of dangerous turns. I had survived one shameful misfortune after another, all of which, individually and together, had left me insensible and deranged. What I did not tell the crowd tonight was that before my miraculous conversion to sanity, it was my aim to find the source of my troubles, the person responsible for my downtrodden condition, a certain Madame Perle Goldenberg who, as far as I knew, had become the wife of a certain wonder rabbi, a Rabbi Eleazar of Chelmno, and who I blamed for all of my earthly woes. After one misadventure and then another, my search brought me at last to Rabbi Eleazar's court in Poland. I had traveled many miles under the most horrible conditions to find Perle Goldenberg. If you saw me at that time you would have wondered, who is that ghost, that vampire, for truly in those days I was barely alive.

"By the time I arrived at Reb Eleazar's court, I was not only exhausted but enraged. I had come to exact revenge on this *rebbitzen*, and not with words or slander. No, my intention was to kill this *rebbitzen*, to murder her with my bare hands."

I must have pulled back from Sara Koblentz, for she put a gentle finger upon my cheek and said, "You've nothing to fear from me, Miss Davidovich. My homicidal days are long behind me. However, at that particular point in time, my desire to destroy the *rebbitzen* ruled my very heart. Little did I know that God had done my work for me. For as I will tell you, I arrived too late.

"When I came upon Reb Eleazar's court, there were pilgrims there from every part of Europe. I thought it was a special holiday, the great rabbi's birthday perhaps. Dozens of hideous little men dressed in fur hats and gabardines, with long side locks and beaded beards, danced about the courtyard. As they spun in circles, their women stood waiting in a long line outside the rabbi's door. I pushed my way through the crowd and banged heavily against it. A man in a fur *strimmel* came to answer. I composed myself as best I could, but it made no difference, for the *shammes* looked right past me. 'I have come to see the *rebbitzen*,' I said.

"'You and every other woman in Poland,' he answered gruffly. 'Stand in line now and wait your turn.'

"'I cannot wait. I have traveled thousands of miles for just this moment,' I whispered, and with a strength I did not know I had, I pushed past the *shammes* and burst into the *rebbitzen*'s chambers. Oh, what I would do to her when I got my hands around her neck! How I would make her pay for all the sorrow and humiliation I had endured so that she might become rich! And so imagine my surprise when I struggled past the guard to find not the *rebbitzen* at all but only a coffin, just her size, sitting in the middle of the room. And bent over the coffin, in a posture of unrelenting grief, was the most elegant woman I have ever seen in my life. So astonishing was she that even in the midst of my frustrated fury I lost my breath looking at her. In addition to her black mourning clothes she wore a fur hat like those of the men in Rabbi Eleazar's court. And this—"

"—was the princess," I whispered.

"Exactly," Sara Koblentz nodded gravely. "So extraordinary was this woman's beauty, so radiant was she, I immediately forgot my disappointment that my long vendetta had been for nothing. Don't ask me why or how, but in this woman's presence, all thoughts of revenge left me. They were replaced almost instantly with a sense of new desire."

I looked down and noticed that I was grasping Sara Koblentz's hand in my own. "What happened next? If you left with the princess, I'm not sure I want to know it."

"Anna Davidovich, how can you not know it? Of course I followed her and of course we made love. But wait. I must tell you how it happened and why...

"First you must understand that up until that moment, I had wandered the earth in a kind of stupor. I had but one thought: to find this *rebbitzen* and murder her. She had stolen my youth and beauty— you heard it from my own mouth just this evening. But when I saw Princess Eugenia, she looked even more downtrodden than I. Not down at the heel mind you, nor crazed, but utterly dejected, and this combined with her extraordinary beauty and obvious wealth woke me to new possibilities. I may have been deranged but I was still crafty, and the thought that this woman might somehow rescue me financially or otherwise shook me out of my bitterness."

"You tricked the princess out of her fortune?"

Sara Koblentz put a finger to my lips and bade me be still. "As you know, Princess Eugenia has very little on her mind besides her own needs. She watched me as I looked from her to the *rebbitzen*'s coffin, and shook her head. 'Disappointing, isn't it, to travel all this way for the *rebbitzen*'s wisdom, only to find her dead.' Then she gazed at me with eyes that were not warm so much as they were resigned. 'Look at you, depraved as well as sorrowful. I cannot face the world alone. I beg of you. Come to lunch.'

"Whether the princess was out to do a good deed—as I have said, I looked a fright and had obviously climbed out of an enormous dung heap—or whether she was hoping for some other kind of communion, I do not know for certain. But I glanced one more time at the *rebbitzen*'s casket, and I stared at the princess, and even in my depraved state I knew on which side my bread was buttered. In a few minutes' time I found myself in the back of a motor car drinking whisky out of Princess Eugenia Vanstazia's silver flask.

"We had not driven half a kilometer when she looked me squarely in the eye. 'I don't imagine you speak Hebrew?' she asked.

"I wasn't sure I heard her correctly. 'Speak Hebrew?'

"'Just the prayers.'"

With that I could keep silent no longer. "She knew the prayers! I taught her the prayers!"

"Oh, Anna Davidovich, of course you did. Of course you taught her the prayers. Princess Eugenia uses the Hebrew prayer book as a kind of prop in an emotional confidence game."

"I don't know what you're talking about." I was truly perplexed. "If you were so badly off, what could she possibly take you for?"

Sara Koblentz ran a hand across my breasts and pushed the hair off my face. Then she leaned over and kissed my forehead. "What indeed. I know I'm a little worn out, my dear, but with a little imagination, you can see that even as a complete wreck I'm not at all unattractive."

I stared at my new friend, not sure whether I should leap up out of my chair or pull Sara down onto my lap. "You are saying that the princess—"

Sara Koblentz kissed me on the mouth and lingered over me for a minute, then she sat back in her own chair. "I am saying that the princess' goyish sexual appetites seem to be more than a little connected to the way we Jewish women speak to God. At any rate, when Princess Eugenia asked me a second time if I knew the Hebrew prayers, I said, 'Of course.'

"'Then you must teach me,' she whispered."

"But I already taught her!" I was outraged, and now I nearly did fly out of my chair.

Sara Koblentz rolled her eyes and stroked my hair. "Calm down, Anna Davidovich. Our princess has a very strange memory. Mine, though dulled at times by too much drink and opium, is actually quite good. And I wasn't above whispering back to her the simple prayer I knew for blessing the Shabbes candles."

"That prayer does seem to have a kind of romantic power over her—" I hissed.

"For myself, I didn't care one way or the other which prayer the princess wanted to know. I was exhausted and perfectly willing to take advantage of whatever consolation we could mutually provide. In time, she had her driver stop at a small hotel just outside Warsaw. The driver opened the door for us and she ushered me to her room. It was a modest room, but it was very well stocked with fishes and fruit and a magnum of wine. She drew me a bath and laid out a satin robe—"

"You got a robe—I was made to be her *morah* in exchange for caviar only."

"That wasn't what the princess told me."

"What did she tell you? What did she say about me?"

Sara leaned over me and stroked my hair. Then she put a finger to my lips and continued. "I asked her what she wanted from me. 'Because if it's what I think you want, I always get paid.'"

"'I want you to tell me about God,' said the princess, and that was all she said.

"After my bath I ate her fruit and caviar, I drank her wine. 'I don't know much about God, nor do I believe in him. I do know the *rebbitzen* was a charlatan.'

"'Oh, the *rebbitzen*,' said the princess, 'how disappointing to find her dead.' Then she leaned over and kissed me like this."

The next morning I awoke with Sara Koblentz in my bed. We had gone up the back stairs to my brother's apartment and somehow made it down the hallway to my room without attracting the least attention. I knew I had not dreamed the evening because both of us were naked. Her dress lay in a heap on the floor, and mine was stuffed at the bottom of the bed. For all my experience with married ladies and then the princess, I had never had the pleasure of any lover being with me in the morning when I woke. I did not have the slightest idea how to behave, and yet I knew full well.

I got up out of bed carefully so as not to awaken my guest. After I washed and dressed, I went into my closet and found my carpetbag and brought it with me into the study. I was pleased to see all my lovers' trinkets wrapped up just as I had left them after the boat ride from Poland. I retrieved the princess' prayer book, and with it the letter I wrote in my stateroom but never mailed. This letter, I crumpled into a tiny ball. Then, on a piece of my brother's new American stationery, with a fine fountain pen he likely won in a card game, I wrote: *Princess Eugenia, I have found this among my possessions and must send it back. I wish you well in your spiritual journey. All the best, I remain, Anna Davidovich.*

I tucked the new letter into Princess Eugenia's prayer book, wrapped and addressed it, then walked down to the street and posted it. I stopped by my shop, told the girl who was baking that I was taking the day off. I collected two fresh sweet rolls and went back home. I woke my new friend with a series of kisses, steaming coffee made the Polish way, and the rolls. After we made love a second time, I asked her quite frankly how long she would be in New York. "Miss Pappenheim leaves for Germany in a few days, but I am to stay here and work for our cause in America."

"Then I must show you New York."

Sara Koblentz held me in her arms. "But first you must teach me the Hebrew prayers."

I looked at her stricken, just for a moment, and then, for the first time in many months, I laughed.

FEAR

Randye Lordon

There was something wrong with the exit door closest to me. Everyone had to turn and use the door at the front of the plane. I was still sitting there, still strapped in my seat, when I saw this little boy standing in the aisle. He couldn't have been more than four, cute as a button and not the least bit frightened. He was amazing; he seemed completely calm. I heard a woman's frantic voice screaming, "Scottie! Scottie," and I saw him turn and try to find the body attached to the voice. But it was impossible. By then, black smoke was filling the airplane and someone in the back was shrieking that fire had broken out. Well, I tell you, as soon as I heard that I jumped out of my seat and went to grab for him, but I was too slow. Once the word *fire* was uttered, the people in the back of the plane panicked. They all surged forward and he went down. I saw the whole thing. I saw the child fall, and then the man behind him—who knew the boy was down—he just kept on barreling ahead, hell-bent on reaching the exit no matter what was in his way.

People are funny, aren't they? I mean, how much time would it have cost him to reach down and pick up that little angel? He had time to grab onto the aisle seats to hop over the child but he couldn't help him up? Clearly no one behind the man realized they were stepping on a child; as far as they knew, he could have been their own carry-on luggage. I mean you can't blame *them,* because well, hell, these people were scared. This thing could have been about to blow the hell up. But I will tell you the truth, as far as I'm concerned there is only one person here guilty of murder, and it's that man. And yes, I know he's denied it; I watched him in the courthouse and on TV and I've seen how he plays to his audience, but I saw what I saw. I know what he did. You know, doing something wrong and owning up to it is one thing. But doing something wrong, like this guy, and pretending like you're innocent is just plain crap. I will lay you any odds that just like OJ, Mr. I-Didn't-Do-Anything-Wrong will one day drive himself absolutely stark-raving mad, which would be perfect justice. Lord knows we are a society that needs to feel we mete out justice, like there could be justice for that kind of thing— a grown man deliberately sacrificing a kid to save his own sorrowful ass.

Anyway, because no one would let me out of my seat and into the aisle, by the time I reached the boy, almost everyone was past him. Even his mother. She had no idea that she'd been part of the stampede that killed him, though I was screaming at her as she went by. I even tried to grab at her, but the woman was like my cousin Teeny— once she gets started on something, there is no way to stop her. I remember one time, it was summer and Teeny and me were at the pool with Aunt Tushy-Bubbles, cause we were spending the week with her. Well, Teeny got it in her mind that she wanted to jump off the high diving board. Now she couldn't have been more than seven years old and eight inches tall, but she was not going to be stopped and that was all there was to that. The second Bubs wasn't looking, that little thing scooted up the ladder and went flying off the board before you could even point at her. Fool didn't even know how to swim. I asked her later, what was she thinking—didn't she know she couldn't swim? She said, "Of course I knew I couldn't swim, I just didn't know I couldn't fly." Right then and there I realized there was something wrong with her. But oh, she pissed me off. When she said she didn't know she couldn't fly I got up in her face and asked her just which one of the divers she'd seen that day had flown? Well, of course she said none because none of them did, but then without batting an eyelash she looked me square in the eye, leaned in real close to me, and practically whispered in my ear, "But there's always a first time, isn't there?"

I still can't stand her.

Oh my Lord, just smell those crabcakes. Mmm-mmm-mm, does that smell like heaven, or what? I am convinced that God himself created the first recipe for crabcakes. It's a funny thing, I don't like any other fish. I mean fish has always given me the willies. As a matter of fact, I was so afraid of fish that I have never once swum in the ocean, and to the best of my recollection, I have managed to steer clear of most lakes. And it's not like I would eat a crab that looked like a crab, you know? I just don't get the attraction. I mean things like squid are positively prehistoric; I don't know how anybody could put anything like that anywhere near their mouths, but they do. I had a roommate once who loved raw oysters. Can you think of anything more revolting than to scrape an oozing life form out of its shell and suck it down? I cannot. I mean I watch people eat them and the only thing I can imagine is a hand or a claw coming out of the sky, plucking my house right off its foundation, prying off the roof, and slurping me and my family down in one terrifying instant. There are just some foods people ought not to eat, like brains. Food like that is enough to make a person a vegetarian. But if you really want to know the truth, I think the cannibals were onto something. Let's face it, people are, for the most part, as disappointing a species as ever there was, don't you think? I think if we ate each other and left God's innocent creatures alone, then the order of things would be in better shape. That man *deliberately* stepped over that little boy, but because the world thinks *I'm* crazy, because they think I was the one responsible for the whole mess, he is able to walk away from what he did and clap his hands together like, *I'm done with this.* In a perfect world that man would be an appetizer.

That little boy—I am telling you, the moment I saw that child I knew he was an angel who had been sent down as an omen to me.

When I finally reached him, I thought I was going to die the smoke was so thick, and indeed I could have sworn I saw flames at the back of the plane, too, but I wasn't afraid. I got on my hands and knees and crawled around until I found him, maybe five feet up from where he fell, half under a seat. There was a stewardess behind us; she was the one who told the police and the media that I was a hero that day. I think maybe if it wasn't for her, I could have actually flown far away from here and saved myself…but no, I guess not. If I had really wanted to do that, I would have.

See, truth is, I set out to conquer my fears, and I did that, which was why I had to volunteer the information that the explosion was my fault, that I was to blame for the whole fiasco. To me things like flying and public bathrooms, ferris wheels and projectile vomiting had always been such overwhelming fears that I was at the point where I was stuck until I dealt with it all. I will forever and always be indebted to Frieda, because with her help I was able to tackle all the items on my list. Each and every thing. And contrary to who people *think* I am, I am not crazy, and I tell you I have never been afraid of myself. I have never been afraid of who I will see when I look in the mirror, because I know even though I have known fear, I am honest and compassionate—which is a fat lot more than I can say for most of the people I have met throughout this ordeal.

I know I'm not the horrible person everyone else believes I am. I know by their silence what my mother and my sister and friends who *said* they used to love me think about me now, but I did what I had to do to triumph over my fears so I could move on with my life. I know what I did was wrong, and I know I deserve to be punished for what I did, but if you believe in justice, if you are even minutely concerned with the soul, then you will understand that that little boy, that darlin' little innocent, died not because of me but because of that man, plain and simple.

You know I have had plenty of time to think about things here, what I did and what happened as a result of my actions, and I realize that there was only one thing I ever really should have been afraid of. People. See, people were at the root of almost every fear I had, including flying, loud noises, public telephones and bathrooms, the Middle East, salmonella, explosions, subways, cancer…you know they say there's a cure for cancer and AIDS, but that the government and the pharmaceutical companies have been able to suppress that information. Now, I would believe that, wouldn't you? Good God, imagine the state of the economy and overpopulation if a cure did exist? A handful of men decide what will and will not be made available to the public—essentially who will live and who will die—and yet, I'm the one people point to in horror. I don't get it. You want to know what I fear? I fear that the meek will never inherit this earth. I fear that the egocentric bullies and cowards will ultimately cause Armageddon. I fear that this planet, which had such great potential, will be completely obliterated because of mankind. I fear that good will forever be overwhelmed by evil. I fear that…

I'm afraid of the electric chair. Isn't that a hoot? I get this far and I'm still afraid. You tell me now, do you really believe that if I ask your forgiveness—and you give it to me—that when you walk out of here I won't be afraid? Because I don't think you have that kind of power. I think you are just a man who has a job representing God—no, not even God, but rather the church, and in my mind the church is one of the biggest, richest manipulators in the world and will probably play a vital role in who presses what button to bring an end to this whole beautiful planet. I mean I know you meant well by coming here to see me, but really, do you have any idea how many wars have been waged by men in the name of God? How many people have died because men like to think they represent the Lord Almighty when in fact these same men just want to be God? So, father, unless you can guarantee that I will feel no fear as I am walked to the room where I will be strapped into a chair where they will cover my head and shoot a billion volts of electricity through me, unless you can promise that, then I am sorry but I cannot ask your forgiveness.

And now, I'm afraid I'll have to ask you to leave.

THE PEARL FISHERS

LINDA NELSON

No eye, or ear, or nose, or tongue, or body, or mind;
No form, no sound, no smell, no taste, no touch, no object of mind.

from *The Prajnaparamita*

THE MEETING, 1995

HELEN

And so Jack took me, finally, home.

This didn't happen without a lot of urging on my part. We'd been on several dates; it had been close to eight weeks since we'd met at the philharmonic. I was tired of drinking coffee and martinis and brushing against his dark sleeve as we stared at modernist paintings together. I learned Jack was particularly fond of Klee, but that he also loved the darkness of Rothko and Reinhardt.

I have, in fact, learned much about Jack already, and, while his stories of himself and where he comes from and how he got to New York leave me oddly uneasy at times, they've also added fuel to my desire for him. His beardless, olive-skinned face is nearly gaunt, as if his thoughts themselves wrench the skin over his cheekbones. He reminds me of a bird of prey. Wild thing that he appears to me to be, I dream of ways to wound him so that I might bring him into my home and nurse him back to health.

Ava's stories, too, had left me uneasy but intrigued.

Perhaps it has something to do with the moral invective which seems to lurk beneath the surface of both Ava's and Jack's tales; they always appear to be trying to achieve something in the telling. As if they wished to make fables from their autobiographies, fables to save me. Or, in Jack's case, fables to save himself and, through himself, the world.

The day with Ava in the library comes to me over and over, a blue hallucination. Perhaps because it was so prescient. It's as if it is a physical shape—a curve or a hill—that was added to my consciousness twenty years ago.

Ava liked to corner girls in the library.

Just what do you think you're doing? was her salutation to me.

I stared in fascination at the long cords of her neck, tough and bronzed as if her most recent vacation was a medal she had pinned to her esophagus. Her neck was a rigging from which to swing her fashionable cowl neck sweaters, those tokens of her success. I remember her elbows seeming to stab randomly at the air, each piece of her as disjointed from the other as a marionette's. Entranced, I wondered if this is what happens over the years, if time indeed acts like the middle pole in a circus tent around which everything spins until one is pulled apart, transformed into a loose sculpture of wooden pieces abandoned by the side of the road.

I was a high school junior when she first pinned me. The library's blond wood shelves, their edges rubbed soft by the hips and shoulders of students just like me, adoring the books while seeking to edge themselves away from her, sought protectively to embrace me. The titles I sought out along the books' spines were my totems. *The Song of the Lark. Siddhartha.* I imagined myself touring Tuscany, collecting images for the editorials I would write for the Sunday paper's

Parade magazine: everything pretty, so pretty, drenched in yellow. And aged: I have always wanted to be old, to not have to live through the doing of the things that need to be done in a life. To be Ava.

She advanced toward me. I could only manage a weak, drifty-eyed smile in her direction.

I believe her gray eyes widened as she grew closer. Her hand shot straight out from her hip, a hand with oversized black and white knuckles flashing out to grab me just above the elbow. A teacher's grab for a student. I didn't want to resist but I did so anyway, playing my part.

In truth, my elbow was boneless, jellylike. Marijuana had happily melted my infrastructure. I was a silly Love Canal, emitting toxins to a disco beat.

Ava propelled me and I danced clumsily before her. She pushed me into a tiny conference room off the library and closed the windowed door behind us. Laurie, Kirsten, and Lisa already sat there, waiting patiently.

The space was reminiscent of something that would only become familiar to me after meeting Jack: a pool table in a too-small bar. There was not enough room around its edges to maneuver a cue or wait one's turn in comfort. Ava squashed me into the chair at the head of the table, and thanks to my gelatinous nature I sank into the awkward space. She then sat beside me, from which vantage she could look through the wire-mesh reinforcement of the door's window, keeping an eye out for other wayward girls. Or for the principal.

The principal, oddly, had become my champion. You're like a daughter to me, McKenna had said, his gray-suited arm and preternaturally flushed face filling my vision. I was sitting in his small, beige office, an enclosure which I believed to be as near to the inside of a filing cabinet as I would ever come in this life.

How I loved to hear those words. Here was a man who was actually more than good to me, more than the benign presence of my father waving good-bye from his recliner, never asking where I was headed as he dangled the remote control in his other hand. The principal was a man who wanted to give me something. And I'd done nothing to earn this honor.

I remember his hugging me roughly, closely. How my side tingled as my skin tried to withdraw and advance simultaneously. Maybe it was simpler than I had realized. Maybe he'd wanted not to give me encouragement but to have something of me, something like my clarinet teacher who had pressed his full worn lips to mine and laughed his boozy jazz down my constricted throat. But I didn't think so then. McKenna went to mass and sat beside my mother. He believed in my intelligence, my goodness.

Ava had assembled her acolytes. The anointed ones—the ones who professed to her their belief in perfection, who gathered around her gospel of achievement. The ones to whom she awarded plaques in honor of elderly local spinsters for things such as "altruistic and inspiring leadership." I desired to be one of them just as much as I despised them. They already had the boys they would marry, and the currencies on which they would stake their claims and live their lives.

Perhaps this first public initiation was just Ava's way of expressing guilt for all our scotch-drenched nights together, for those moments when her hand slipped from the back of the couch to my sweaty neck. More likely she took pleasure from wrestling McKenna for my soul. So many of them tried, tried to get their hands around and into that slippery, intangible part of me. As if my body were not enough.

And now Jack.

None of the acolytes could look at me. Their hands stayed in their laps beneath the pale wood table. Their breasts brushed its edge, alert, betraying their gratitude for being among the jury and not the accused.

You are squandering everything, Ava hissed.

Laurie raised her wide eyes to mine. Everything, she repeated in a sweetly trained whisper.

Who will ever marry you? Lisa wondered. Smoking dope with those boys in the alley.

Ava cut her eyes at Lisa, then nodded at Kirsten, who spoke the critical line: Who will ever take you?

I have given you everything, Ava concluded.

Repent! Repent! My little angels sang in the blue unisphere round my head.

I giggled uncontrollably.

It was Ava—not one of the girls, with whom I had learned this technique in public speaking class—who slammed the side of her hand down on the table top.

Squander! Waste!

I stared off above their heads. The marijuana lightly coated my vision, softening and blending the four of them into a perfect unity. In the yellow haze, I read my future: the road was wide and straight, passing through miles of nothing with the sun setting at its end. A topography unlike anything I'd encountered in my east coast childhood. My efforts to change this scene brought a scowl to my face. Why not long tweed skirts and gold rings, billowing blouses and iambic pentameter?

The days of equal rights—in the form of a proposed amendment, green-and-white 59 CENTS buttons (to indicate a woman's wage in relation to a man's dollar), and the National Organization for Women were fully upon us in 1978. Within this context, I was already a new kind of American heretic: she who might spurn career enticements and future earning potential for the lure of more hedonistic, less lofty, goals.

This is my blood, drink from it.
This is my body, eat of it.

And so Jack took me home.

We never turned on the lights. From the stories he had told me, I imagined many things: a collection of old carnival handbills, a four-poster bed, windows opening high above the river. But the apartment was dark in a way I'd never understand, and it was as if Jack soaked it into himself. He pressed his blackness into me, filled me with it there in the entryway, barely inside the door. The floor was slick beneath my icy ass, and suddenly I wished he had told me none of his stories.

JACK

I do not allow people into my home, but for Helen I made an exception.

Her white hair was fire in reverse, her skin chill as if emptiness burned inside her. I imagined I was stealing her away from her father, Agamemnon, and her other suitors.

Before I could take her inside, there was much for which I had to prepare her.

The only thing I would not tell her before bringing her into the apartment was what had finally propelled me east. That I would reserve for later, for once I had her there.

And so, in the weeks after our fateful meeting, I told her my lies: how as an adolescent I'd decided to fly east into the face of the sun, leaving behind the few people who knew me, running from the prickly reflectivity of the desert and its lack of shadows. How I did this and made of myself a poet, fashioned in the New York, bohemian school, charming academic colleagues at cocktail parties in rambling upper-west side apartments. How next I made of myself a painter, splashing my feelings over the sides of bars and galleries, pinwheeling my soul in bright colors across the city. There was a truth in these tales to which I could not admit. How I did make something of myself: a gift to all the beautiful women I met. A gift to give Helen.

But at this point, how to tell the rest? How to tell her that this was a dream my best friend Michael and I had had together, and how one ecstatic, frantic night between a young dyke and a younger fag had denied us it forever? How to tell her this when she so innocently adores Jack? How to explain the daughter I left in L.A.?

Instead, I made up a story for her, the way I tell stories to myself. I told her the story of Jack's trip, state by state, across the south-western U.S.

In the story of Texas, Jack was a hero in a diner, saving the waitress from rape at the hands of truckers and wreaking humorous, if bloody, revenge upon them.

In Oklahoma, Jack chased shots of peppermint schnapps with Budweiser at a cocktail bar and seduced a dark, local beauty who had just emerged from a year's hospital rehabilitation due to a nearly fatal car crash. In Jack's arms on the dance floor, the left foot this vixen would drag for the rest of her days floated smoothly to old Glenn Miller tunes.

Jack stayed too long in Arkansas, rescuing Emma from an abusive partner and living in her paneled trailer in its meager stand of pine, coaxing and making love to her terror until she was ready to face the world again.

I didn't tell Helen that I would have chosen to remain in that tiny, isolated trailer had not Emma kicked me out. To stay where I belonged.

As each state passed, the myth of Jack grew in size with the miles I had put behind me.

In Virginia, by a sparkling stream in the Blue Ridge Mountains, outside a potter's barn, Jack and I saw that everything is empty. We had found our god.

But Helen is uninterested in all of this. She doesn't need it: I am already the hero for whom she has been looking. She has latched onto me as her way out of something I can't quite define. But I can expand into her emptiness, and it is exactly this I seek.

The story she most likes me to retell is of my arrival into New York.

How I rumbled across the still relatively new Verrazano Narrows bridge wailing Woodie Guthrie—"From California, to the New York Island..."—and, working my way down the twisted ramp into Bay Ridge, Brooklyn, finally pulled over, exhausted, to gape across the harbor. Liberty waved greenly to me from above the yellow double-decker Staten Island ferry on which my father's mother had told of riding. The rich platinum skyline of my dreams rose fierce and quill-like on the horizon.

The pleasing stink of the Narrows blew warmly across my face. I described to Helen how I had listened to the roar of the Belt Parkway ten feet behind me, as rhythmic as the waves of the Pacific crashing at the feet of the oil pumpers at Long Beach. A tiny passenger ferry tootled into the harbor beneath the generous giganticism of the bridge. Its steady throb filled the measures between the glissando of oncoming cars as it moved from one channel marker to the next, keeping the red buoys to its starboard side.

I told Helen how I had felt my own sweat dripping, leaving a trail of salty white down the back of my neck. And how it was then, streaked with salt and miles and fear, that I knew I would now be somebody entirely different from the person I had been born in Los Angeles. I had arrived at the next big thing. Here, in New York, I could be my own experiment, my own monster.

I was thrilled. My transformation had begun my last night in L.A. I didn't recognize myself as I flew down out of the tree, agile and stealthy as Batman. There in the shadow I felt it. Fastening my arm beneath Freya's shoulders, I heaved her up from where she bent so terribly over John.

I had escaped from the cemetery. I had made it to New York. After watching Freya hobble lopsidedly but swiftly down the dark hill, a Lon Chaney staggering after the bullet for which I'd wrestled grazed her thigh, I never saw her again.

I told Helen how, that morning on the harbor's edge, I'd begun to count the boats: a small private fishing boat, a tanker, a boat named the Riptide brimming with shouts and laughter. I had glanced over at my Bel Air and been amazed we had made it so many miles. As if its namesake, that sweet pocket of air between Malibu and the Hollywood Hills, had borne us three thousand miles together.

But it was the seabirds flocking at the boats' sterns and not the boats themselves which ultimately captured my attention. None of them was familiar to me, none related to the flocks of indistinguishable little brown birds which had surrounded me and my people in the dusty hills northeast of Los Angeles. *Las avitas morenas.*

The one that drew me was a long, dark shape with a ropy, extended neck. It flapped its wings so close to the surface, I thought surely it was sick. Its feathers looked gluey, stuck together as if it had been caught in an oil spill, and it seemed to me to be blind, its eyes, too, dissolved by some terrible chemical accident. It was a horrific sight amid the carnival of birds, and I averted my face, wondering if it was a sign that I should continue my journey, go further north, keep moving.

Smaller, startlingly white birds with sharp black caps and long forked tails rose and fell beside the sick bird as if on an amusement park ride to the sea. Through the arc of their wings I glimpsed a tall metal tower and the low skeleton of a roller coaster. Coney Island! The promise of this surreal heaven lured me from this skyful of evil omens, and I trotted back to the car and merged into heavy eastbound traffic.

When the famed boardwalk clattered under my feet, with all its loose nails and missing planks and dangerous holes gaping to the dark beneath, when the smell and sizzle of cheap cooking oil and cotton candy curled into my hair, I knew I would stay. I wove through green wire trash barrels and clots of people, listening to the ball game from someone's pocket transistor. The Mets were up, having a good year in 1967. The beach was crowded but nothing like the photos I'd seen from the turn of the century, when tens of thousands of pale, heavyset people were packed, fat arm to fat arm, beside each other along the narrow beach.

A tiny Chinese woman raised her flowered rain umbrella to protect her from the sun; a group of women bulged over and around the constraints of neon-hued halters; a Middle Eastern woman, layered in dark gauzy cloth, determinedly steered her children along. Another woman wore the number of a Yankee star stretched tightly across her back; yet another surprised everyone with a lime green string bikini and exposed, jiggling buttocks. Women in hot pants hugged to their chests cheap stuffed animals somebody had won for them. I told Helen how happy they had all made me.

At the end of that first day, as the sun set and chilly shadows raced people wheeling their belongings to the subway along the walk, I heard a woman's voice: watch the baby, he's got a gun! Her tone was completely normal. Seconds later, three uniformed police thundered past. I froze. But no one scattered. I stood unseeing as the crowd moved around me, no one reacting any differently to the notion of a gun than to that of a basketball or a stroller.

But I'd held one in my hands, held it hot and recently. Smelled it. Felt the bullet ripped from its barrel. The searing, the screaming.

When the sun had slipped away, the sky was a dangerous orange. In L.A., the day doesn't burn out like this; instead it becomes a soft gray, softer and softer until the buildings of downtown fade into the lights of Dodger Stadium, which perches like a lit crown between the valley and the city.

Telling Helen this, I had a startling moment—the first in nearly twenty years—of missing the summer night air of the Pacific, the way it spreads and rustles its wings. The way the mockingbirds plagiarize wildly, late, late, while cars roar west along Sunset Boulevard to the sea.

THE TRIP, 1967

Jack

I knocked my coffee spoon off the counter and left the stool spinning. The spoon bounced to the floor with the sound of cell bars clanging shut.

I was nineteen years old and on my way through Texas, and my long legs chewed up the distance to the door of the diner in barely three steps. Before the waitress could reemerge from the kitchen, I leapt into my car without bothering to check the trunk. Despite the wall of water the storm seemed to lower on me, the ignition turned over quickly and smoothly.

I had my arm over the passenger seat and was backing out of the lot in a big, fast arc that tested the torque of my bearings when I saw headlights approaching. I rammed the long chrome lever on the steering column up too fast, missing drive and throwing the car into neutral. Gravel flew from beneath the rear tires as my engine raced and everything screamed. The headlights, blurred in the gray downpour, grew closer. I wasn't sure what the waitress had seen, but I knew what I had left behind me in L.A. and I was afraid.

The headlights that night in the cemetery had been, unlike these, as sharply clear as the wounds that had been inflicted.

John stood in the full wash of this light, looking for all the world like Hamlet about to launch into his soliloquy, his chin pointed high as he tried to locate us in the tree's branches.

I know you're up there! he repeated, although this time his voice quavered slightly. Freya, they've told me what you two girls do!

The music from the Asteroid stopped. I remember feeling the car exhale, settling into a shuddering silence.

Freya had, like me, remained motionless to this point. But then I heard the latch of one of the car's doors release, saw the door's opening widen, a booted foot begin to emerge.

Using the same hand with which I had grabbed the branch below me that night, I found the shift lever and moved it into drive. The headlights slowed and turned into the diner beside me, showing the brown-and-yellow star of a Texas sheriff. The car pulled carefully up to the wall of the diner as I turned onto the blacktop. Glancing back,

I saw its headlights dim as the driver unfolded himself and headed up the steps and through the door.

What had I wanted in that tree? A mere week had gone by, and already I couldn't remember. Freya had been lovely and golden, yet I had hardly been aware of her. Gripping the tree between my thighs and riding the high heavens of the Hollywood Hills, my mind and body still burning with the memory of the baby I had not wanted and would never see again, I ground my stitches into the rough bark.

The road sang giddily beneath my tires as I steered the car east. It already seemed so far away. In twenty years, I'd probably feel as if the story was one I'd invented. For as long as I'd been growing up in L.A., I'd wanted to move to New York. I hated the West in all its newness and glitter, hated the spotlights that stroked the sky outside Grauman's Egyptian Theater on opening nights, the starlets who stretched their haunches for their caress as they stepped from long, wide cars. Hated the sound of rain crashing down on the metal roof of our tiny church and rushing, if only briefly, the cement walls of the L.A. River. I longed for streets too narrow for limos, crooked village streets as I'd only read about in Millay's poems; for the swirling gray river and smoking tugs and barges Whitman had described. It was toward this end that Michael and I, laughing, had practiced flattening out our speech, erasing the speedy, clipped inflections which might locate us forever in East L.A. He had always, since the time we were babies and three curls looped across his forehead, been so much prettier than I. Finally, even his cock so surprisingly beautiful to me, a smooth purple jumping with its own desires. And so we matched each other, his prettiness to my strength, these things so needy of each other.

Glancing in the rearview mirror proved no one was behind me. I didn't need to stop to check the trunk: I remembered the lovely shredding of the trucker's trousers with my razor as what it was, a fantasy. I patted my jeans pocket. Sure enough, the razor was still there, slim and tightly closed. It had been rusted shut since the day I'd salvaged it from the river into which I'd watched my brother throw it. Throwing away this part of himself that I wanted to remember.

My hand around the razor, I heard the echo of his voice, thick, rancid, jeering at us as Michael and I had sat poring over a book of photographs of New York.

Don't you know people in the East all want to come West? You two have it backward. Miguel! This is where the future is.

I will always see blood. Blood on everything I touch. The wounds etched as stringently as tattoos the length of John's neck and chest. The way his white flesh split and reddened in the dancing particles of the Asteroid's headlights. How I had grabbed the gun in the hand of the Asteroid's pale passenger just as it went off, and then pulled Freya away from where she had made ribbons of John's chest with no less skill than a lioness. The oddness of watching her be swallowed by the darkness while the Asteroid claimed its passengers and disappeared as well, leaving me hovering above the body like a soul abandoned.

This is the future. Does it matter who piloted the razor, who pulled the trigger? I thought one last time of the trucker, of how fashionably I had imagined slicing his jeans into fringes, leaving them to hang from his belt like a hippie hula skirt whirling round the maypole of his penis. I was halfway to my destination, free and halfway to my life's next great story.

SHADOW LINE

ELISABETH NONAS

P eter was my only friend who knew me from the days of my
Hollywood failure. He was already sick when he and Ethan
met four years earlier. They were my best friends. My L.A.
family. Well, basically my only family. My parents were dead
and I had no siblings, only distant cousins who lived in places
like Minneapolis and Syracuse, New York, and who tended to visit
during winter months if at all.

Peter and Ethan lived in a house in the hills above Sunset, on Queens
Road. We joked about that a lot. They knew several other gay cou-
ples near them—we called it Queens Row.

Their place was squeezed onto the hillside, too close to the house
on either side to really notice when you drove up whether it was cute
or dignified or Spanish or just a typical Hollywood Hills house, which
is what it was. More boxy than anything else.

Night-blooming jasmine clustered in thick profusion at the bottom of the steep steps leading to the front door. Luminaria lined the
stairway, and a mix of cacti, succulents, and driftwood greeted visi-

tors at the top.

Despite the flowers and the fragrance and the colors, the house was starting to look different to me, even from the street. Brighter, incandescent almost, as if it were doing its part to keep Peter alive, soaking up all the sun's heat to help warm the body already cooling toward death.

I punched in the code for the alarm and let myself in through the purple wrought-iron gate. Each visit I dreaded the climb. Not because I wasn't fit, but because I hated surprises. And these days I never knew what I was going to find inside.

Pal, Ethan's boxer, was at me before I got through the gate. I let him say hello and sniff at my dog's scent as I walked awkwardly forward.

Ethan greeted me at the door. "Sorry to leave that cryptic message. I was just so upset with this new nurse—he left Peter alone for about half an hour. And he'd just started the morphine drip."

Not a good sign. Peter had been reluctant to go on morphine, believing it signified the beginning of the end. Ethan just wanted Peter to be comfortable. "Is that the other thing you meant in your message?"

"No." He put his hand on my arm to steady me. "Janet's here."

I hid my panic at the mention of Peter's sister's name. Of course it was logical that she'd have come. I tried to be an adult. After all, this wasn't about me. "Is the dick here, too?"

"You mean Richard? Nope, he stayed in Seattle. But she brought the girls. Peter asked to see them."

"And they wanted to come?"

"Apparently they did."

"How long is she staying?" I asked.

Ethan looked at me but didn't say anything. I was being really dense, trying to recover from the shock. Then it hit me—she'd come to say good-bye. She'd leave when Peter died.

"You just missed her. She took the kids back to the hotel. They've been here since breakfast. She's good with him, Zo, it's made a big difference. She'll be over for dinner."

My apprehension at seeing her, even after all these years, surprised me. But more important things were happening, and I'd just have to deal.

We walked through to Peter's bedroom. It used to be their room, but in the last year Ethan had set up a bed in what had been the study because of Peter's late-night I.V. drips, his wandering and restlessness.

Ethan stopped us in the doorway, then pulled me forward so I was next to him. He had confessed to enjoying just watching his lover, not interacting with him, but observing him from a distance, memorizing the tiniest details of their life together. For later.

He had a lot to memorize. Their world changed almost daily. The transformation of illness showed everywhere, not only in Peter's body but in the room itself, as decorative objects became functional, enlisted in service to the transformative process of life moving to death. The accouterments of illness invaded every corner. A blue-and-white Italian ceramic bowl was filled with syringes and gauze and sterile pads, vials and medications. Extra I.V. lines hung off the Oscar on the dresser.

Peter lay on top of the covers. He looked asleep, and something else: relaxed. First time I'd seen him like that in months. I didn't know if it was the visit with his sister or the drugs.

Ethan knocked gently on the doorframe.

Peter opened his eyes and turned toward me. "Did Ethan tell you about the morphine?

I nodded.

"This morning I had another panic attack. I called Ralph, and he said it was time to start." Peter made it declarative, his shrink's orders, but he still held the question in his eyes.

I sat on the edge of the bed near him. "Sounds like a good idea."

"Panic will keep me from experiencing it."

It. His dying.

"If I'm panicked I'm not present."

I stroked his cheek. "You told me you wanted to be present for this."

"I believe I do," he said. Whir of the morphine contraption. He lay back and closed his eyes. Fighting to hold on and beginning to let go at the same time.

Ethan stretched out on the bed next to Peter, careful not to hurt him. "You hungry, lover? Zoë brought dinner." Peter shook his head.

Ethan turned to me. "I'll sit with him for a while. You go ahead without me."

I tiptoed out of the room. I moved quietly around the kitchen, even though I knew any noise I made wouldn't reach back to the bedroom. Being in motion helped. I tried to get mad at Ethan for not telling me about Janet's arrival but I knew I was merely distracting myself. I didn't want to think about her. Janet. Peter's only sibling. Wife, mother of two. The first true love of my life.

Peter had introduced us years before. He was still working swing gang on a TV series. I was a would-be producer, temping in a production office, and in my off hours developing *Sweet Girl*—a feature film, the first of what I hoped would be many I would produce. Janet was waitressing when we met, just breaking even till she figured out what she really wanted to do. At the beginning we went out with Peter and his friends, part of a pack. Being with her was intoxicating, and that had nothing to do with the drugs everyone was doing in those days. She was wild—possessed of a crazy excess energy. I spent more and more time with her.

One evening she'd picked me up at the office, and as we were driving out Santa Monica Boulevard to the beach, we witnessed an accident. A car swerved out into traffic and hit a motorcycle. We couldn't see the bike but watched as the rider and the girl who hung onto his slim hips went flying fifteen feet into the air, somersaulted, and landed on the pavement in front of the car. He landed on his back, she was crawling on hands and knees, wailing.

A lot of pictures are filmed on the streets of L.A., but this wasn't a movie stunt.

We were a few cars back from the collision and were waved on with the rest of the traffic. But I'd frozen. As soon as the screech and thud came, I put my hand on Janet's thigh. An involuntary reaction. I wasn't aware I'd done it until she'd driven a few blocks west. Janet covered my hand with her own, pulled it a bit closer to some very warm part of herself, and applied an insistent pressure. "Life is very short," she'd said.

We went to bed together that night. I realized I'd been in love with her almost since we'd met. She was funny, smart, attractive. She was the sister of one of my best friends. She encouraged my Hollywood dreams. I couldn't separate my professional success from Janet's and my relationship. Both began around the same time. When all the pieces crumbled, I couldn't tell which had broken first.

Janet found a job as a technical writer for a big corporation. She tolerated the work because she loved the salary and the benefits. I didn't begrudge her any of that, since my car leaked when it rained and making the rent was a monthly challenge. In addition, interest in *Sweet Girl* was picking up, and the excitement made up for my temporary—or at least that's how I saw it—cash flow problem. Soon we'd both have good jobs and a life together.

The changes in Janet started out small. Increasingly, she liked her job, talked about her co-workers. She came home suggesting we go to a particular restaurant because "one of the fellows in the office" said it was fabulous. I found the place intolerably stuffy and straight. Janet loved it. She read books people from work lent her. Bought wine on their recommendation. What got to me more than this infatuation with her colleagues was that Janet had to be very closeted at work, and soon this extended to her life outside the office, which meant into my life. We couldn't hold hands in public. She no longer wanted to be seen with Peter and his friends, at least not when I was around.

Don't think I didn't call her on this.

"Zoë," she said, after I'd been at her for an entire Sunday afternoon, "did it ever occur to you that I might want to have children?"

That stopped me. I wanted children, too. This was a terrific thing.

"I can't do that with another woman," she said.

"You wouldn't be doing it with another woman. You'd be doing it with me."

"I can't."

Simple as that. We were over. Sure, it took longer than that one conversation, but not much.

Then her company transferred her to Seattle.

I might have flown up to try to talk her out of it, see if we could salvage us, but my movie was going down the toilet—at least my involvement in it was—and I needed to stay in L.A. if I hoped to remain even remotely connected to the project. We tried the long-distance thing for a little while. In less than a year she'd met and married this guy Richard and was pregnant with their first child.

I refused to let Janet's actions ruin my friendship with Peter. He confided in me that he'd much rather have me for an in-law than this Richard character. But after the wedding I stopped asking for news, and Peter no longer offered.

I moped around for about a year. Drank a lot, slept with a lot of women, and finally went into therapy. I let go of Janet and eventually the film business and reconstructed my life, entered graduate school and worked toward my Ph.D. and becoming a therapist. I enjoyed several happy years until my friends started being diagnosed with HIV. Then my life became a combination of work and loss.

The dog's barking snapped me out of my reverie. I had a carton of take-out in each hand, a dish rag slung over one shoulder, and I'd spilled sesame sauce on my pants. Glamorous.

And there in the doorway stood the woman who'd once been the love of my life.

We faced each other, a butcher block table and a million miles between us.

Something exploded in the microwave just as the timer beeped off and green letters scrolled out E-N-J-O-Y-Y-O-U-R-M-E-A-L. Pasta sauce splattered the inside of the machine.

Janet jumped into action. She grabbed the rag from my shoulder, set a Pyrex dish in front of the microwave, and opened it carefully. As she spooned out the glop she said, "Still handy as ever in the kitchen, huh Zoë."

I tried to sound amused. "It didn't heat up the first time around."

"I hate these things," she said, working efficiently all the while. "Richard bought me one as soon as they came out—'it'll make your life sooo much easier'—and I never use it for precisely this reason."

As she made the dish presentable, she said, "You look good."

I couldn't honestly return the compliment. Not that she wasn't an attractive woman still. But she'd turned into a suburban hyphen-ate—wife-mother—with a healthy tan, no-nonsense haircut, sensible but expensive clothes. I surreptitiously searched for even a hint of the wild gal I'd loved all those years ago; she was nowhere to be found. The transformation angered me. Or my reaction to it did— I thought less of her because she'd chosen this life for herself.

"There," she exclaimed, wiping an extraneous drop of sauce from the lip of the dish. "Not bad."

We each prepared a plate and took it into the living room, but neither of us could eat.

"Ethan said you brought your daughters with you?"

"They wanted to come. Patricia's twelve, Katy's six."

"Do they know why you're here?"

"Patricia does. Katy knows something's up, but is less interested in the specifics." Janet thought about that for a second. "Not that she doesn't love her uncle. I wasn't sure it was a good idea—I didn't know how much they should be exposed to. But Richard is working on a big project and wouldn't have been able to spend much time with them anyway."

That was the second time she'd worked in his name. I tested my reaction to it—not much registered on my emotional meter. This might just go fine. "So where are they now?"

"Back at the hotel. Timothy is sitting with them."

Timothy, the queeniest of Peter and Ethan's friends.

"The girls just love him. He's so patient with Katy, and Patricia likes him even though he loves the dolls as much as Katy. Patricia's going through a tomboy stage. She wants us to call her Jack." Janet laughed. "Richard's furious. He's sure it's Peter's influence...he doesn't know I used to be with women." She glanced quickly at me.

I had too many opinions about that—starting with the deceit on which she'd based her married life. I refused to go there. I'd given her up years before. "Would you have a problem if your daughter turned out to be gay?"

"I'd probably admire her for going through with it." She didn't look at me this time. "For being true to herself."

Precisely the area I wanted to avoid.

Janet shrugged. "I really did fall in love with Richard. And without him I wouldn't have my girls—they're the most wonderful gifts."

I bit my tongue and said nothing. She couldn't quite make eye contact. I didn't believe her for a second. Not about loving her girls— Peter adored them, I'm sure they were wonderful. But Janet talked too fast and too much to be convincing. She talked to let off the nervous discomfort—it was evident in her constant motion, popping up to get salt and pepper, or light the candles, pour each of us more water. Maybe she thought I'd be judging her. Maybe she was right.

"I always admired Peter's life," she said. "Rather, his ability to live it like he had no choice. I see that as true freedom. I've always—"

I didn't get to find out what she'd "always" because Ethan called us and his tone made us run to him.

He was sitting next to Peter, stroking his chest, his cheek. His other hand held Peter's. "I think he's going."

Janet and I fell into position on the other side of the bed. For a second I thought Peter had already died—he hadn't taken a breath since we'd entered the room. But then there came a slow rasp and he inhaled. His chest barely moved. He exhaled. Inhaled again.

The three of us looked at each other, giddy with success, as if we'd somehow been responsible for pulling him back from the brink of death.

Ethan leaned back, fanned his face. "Mary, my nerves!"

This episode introduced us to a new stage in Peter's illness. We didn't know how many more episodes like that we'd have until he finally reached the end. This time now felt like a reprieve, which probably accounted for why the three of us sat in there for another hour, not talking much, content to be in the same room with Peter, listening to his labored-but-even breathing. Where once the conversation would have been lively, nonstop, now this was enough.

It wasn't easy to tear myself away, but I had early morning clients. "Long day tomorrow." I kissed Ethan's cheek. "You can call me anytime."

Janet stood as well. "I'll go too."

She hugged Ethan, kissed Peter's forehead, and we made our way outside.

Janet and I stood at the foot of the steps, sweet scents swirling around us. She looked lost, like she couldn't remember where she'd left her car, or if she even had one, or what city she was in. Coming out of the house was like returning from a trip to some foreign country where the pace and language were different. I always needed a minute to get my bearings, remind myself that the world didn't stop as Peter's life ground to its halt. Janet turned to me then and said,

"I don't know if I can manage driving." And promptly collapsed in tears.

I couldn't make out all she said, but the general gist of it was that we'd almost lost him then and what would happen when we finally did.

I held her while she sobbed. Even after the sounds stopped she still trembled in my arms. My own tears hung back. A few trickled out with Janet's, but mostly I felt numb. My grief waited somewhere else; I couldn't share it with someone I no longer trusted.

Janet pulled away from me, fumbled in her purse for a tissue. "I don't think I really want to go back to the hotel yet. I'm not quite ready to face the girls."

What the hell. I might go home but I'd never get to sleep. "How about a drink?" I offered.

I wasn't about to bring her to my house, so I took us to the bar at the Bel Age hotel. I didn't know which one of us was more uncomfortable. "I don't really drink anymore" was all that she said. What do you order a grief-stricken nondrinking ex-lesbian? Janet was no help. "I'll have whatever you're having."

Taking her at her word, I ordered two Martels.

"Here," I said, passing one of the snifters to her. "This is cognac."

The fumes didn't bother her. She took a rather large gulp. "That's good, thanks," she said. "He looks so much worse than I expected."

"I guess I've gotten used to it," I said. What happens when you watch someone die is that you fit yourself with a corrective lens which enables you to see the debilitated person before you as a direct match for the healthy person you knew. If you haven't seen that person for a while, you haven't been adjusting the lens and could be in for a shock.

"So...you became a therapist," Janet said.

There was so much we weren't saying that conversation was almost impossible. Once I answered yes, there wasn't anywhere to go with that. We chatted. The woman I'd been ready to spend my life with, and here we were, chatting. Could she really be talking to me about the carpool?

"Listen to me go on," she said.

She finished the rest of her drink in two gulps.

"Another?" I asked.

"Please," she said.

By the time she'd downed that one her features had softened a little. She looked even more like Peter when she was relaxed. Or maybe that was because she was crying softly and continuously.

"Forgive me." She searched unsuccessfully in her purse for another tissue. "It's just that...well, you know."

Matter of fact, I no longer had a clue. I handed her a wad of paper napkins from the bar.

"Thank you," she sniffed.

She didn't talk at all as I drove her back to her car.

Constructing one's life around keeping a secret takes a tremendous amount of energy. I couldn't help but compare Janet to Priscilla Townsend, one of my clients, who'd hidden her husband's secret and its consequences on her own life until she could bear it no longer.

Once Priscilla Townsend started talking to me about her disease and the end of her life with her husband, her anger surfaced, then erupted. The release energized her, she said. "I feel better than I have since my diagnosis." She told two of her closest friends that she had AIDS. Their support encouraged her to tell more people. Telling the truth became contagious. Soon she made plans to visit her sons in Northern California. "It's time I told them what's happening. And what happened."

I wondered if Janet would ever be able to face the lie she'd lived all these years. If she even understood the consequences. It wasn't like Edward Townsend's lie to Priscilla. Janet hadn't transmitted a disease to her husband. She hadn't even had an affair. But with her denial she'd cut off a part of herself, truncated her experience and her existence.

I couldn't really afford the time I was spending thinking about this. My practice had exploded in the last few weeks. Clients I hadn't heard from in years called and wanted to come in to deal with some current crisis.

I attributed this revival to the recent article in the paper about my brief involvement in the movie business—people who'd known me only as a therapist were curious about my days in the industry. As I talked to them, I reminded myself of Janet talking about having fallen in love with Richard. I spoke only minimally about my former life, gave my standard rap about how I'd realized I wanted to be doing something productive after I left the business, etc. It's what people wanted to hear. Needed to hear. But it was only a line, I knew. Janet's appearance at Peter's bedside made me question the truth of my own life. Priscilla Townsend's honest emotional search shamed me into foraging around in my own history. Maybe I'd been lying to myself for years, fooled myself into thinking I didn't mind my failure, was content with things as they stood.

Over the next two weeks I spent time at Peter and Ethan's every day. I worked it in whenever I could, swinging by with lunch or a treat mid-afternoon, stopping in for a quick goodnight on my way home. Sometimes Janet was there, sometimes out with the girls. Her nervous veneer had worn off, thank God. She was more subdued. The toll of watching her brother die showed in her eyes, the drawn set of her mouth. She may have changed from when I first knew her, but at least she hadn't become one of those chipper types who covered everything over with a layer of prattle about making the best of the situation, or possibly worse, a continuous stream of euphemisms.

Her daughters were often at the house, and though intimidated by them—what was I supposed to talk about?—I liked the girls the moment I met them. The kids brightened and cluttered up the place. The older one looked a lot like her mother. Katy, the younger, must have taken after the father, though I detected some resemblance to photos I'd seen of Peter when he was young. She was sweetly polite when Janet introduced us.

Patricia, on the other hand, directed her sassy eyes right into mine after we'd been introduced and asked, "Are *you* gay too?"

Perceptive kid. "Yup, I am."

"Patricia," Janet chided, "what have I told you about that?" Janet turned to me. "I'm sorry."

"No need."

When Peter was alert, he liked to visit with his nieces. The routine at the house evolved into the unusual combination of fun and death.

One day Ethan, Janet, and I were going over the phone tree of people to be notified when Peter died. Peter himself had drawn up the list in his stronger days. He knew exactly who he wanted at his funeral. Everything was typed and in alphabetical order, except for a few scratchy pencil additions made more recently. The girls played in the pool. Their gleeful shrieks provided a strange contrast to our indoor activities. I liked the sound, found it comforting.

I watched Janet work. She was very efficient, able to concentrate on more than one task at a time, field phone calls, keep an eye out for the kids, go over people and food lists.

At one point Katy came in, wet bathing suit and dripping feet, cranky and tired, and whispered something in her mother's ear. Janet listened, then hauled Katy—drips and all—onto her lap and continued working while Katy just sat there and rested, big eyes taking everything in until they grew heavy-lidded and fluttered closed. She slept there as Janet worked.

I envied that. I wanted that unconditional love, someone to make me safe and send me back out into the world when I was ready.

I watched my thoughts about Janet flip from the scorn of my first impression of her to a dense and complicated longing. When Ethan said he needed to talk to Janet about Peter's will, I offered to take the kids for lunch. Ethan shot me a quizzical look. He knew how uncharacteristic that was of me. But Janet beamed, as if it signified my acceptance of her life. Maybe it did.

Janet ordered the girls out of the pool and into their clothes. Their disappointment that she wasn't going along was tempered by my promise to put down the top on the convertible.

We piled into the car. "What do you want? I know a really cool place where we can sit outside."

"McDonald's, McDonald's," Katy clamored.

"This restaurant used to be a house that belonged to a movie star." I turned to Patricia as a voice of reason. "Jack?" I asked, in an attempt to win her over as my ally.

If she was surprised that I knew about her preferred nickname, she didn't show it. "McDonald's," she said.

Who was I to argue? I thought, all the while smugly reassuring myself that if I had kids, I'd never let them eat that junk.

I drove us through Laurel Canyon to Studio City where I vaguely remembered they had a McDonald's.

Katy ordered a Happy Meal. I let Patricia order for me, and we both ended up with a Quarterpounder with cheese, large fries, and a Coke.

We brought our food to a table overlooking the parking lot.

"See, we're outside," said Katy.

"We certainly are," I agreed.

The girls opened their various boxes and bags. Jack was good with her sister, helping her with the games on the Happy Meal box, checking to see she wasn't making too much of a mess.

I liked being out with them. I imagined people assuming I was their mother. We ate in silence. I kept looking for traces of Peter in the girls. He adored them. But what did he talk about with them, anyway? Could I learn? Everything I thought to say would have been appropriate for kids visiting L.A. for a vacation—Disneyland, the Universal Studios tour, the beach—not for a death.

Patricia was looking at me. I was afraid she could read my thoughts and deflected by asking, "Your food good?"

Katy nodded enthusiastically and patted her stomach. "Yummy!"

Patricia shrugged. "It's okay. Mom never lets us eat McDonald's."

Katy asked permission to go to the playground around the other side of the restaurant. Jack and I sat at the table in awkward silence.

"How long have you known Uncle Peter?" she finally asked.

"A very long time. Longer than your parents have known each other."

"He has a lot of friends," she said.

"Yes, he does."

"My parents don't have so many friends," she said. "And the ones they do have are boring." She jammed her hands in her pants pockets. "It sucks that he's dying."

"You can say that again, Jack."

Janet thanked me for taking the girls. "How's about I pay you back for that drink?" she asked.

I followed her to the hotel. Janet parked me in her room while she went to the adjoining room to settle the girls in for the night.

She returned a few minutes later. "Okay, about that drink." She leaned over the small refrigerator mini-bar. "There's cognac—a different kind than you ordered."

"Just a soda would be fine. Something diet."

"Should I get some ice?"

"This'll be fine."

She sat at the edge of her bed and studied the label of her drink. "You know that stuff about my husband"—she hadn't been able to call him by his name since that first time she mentioned him—"um, I don't know why I said that. That I fell in love with him. That's the line I give everyone. I almost believe it myself. Truth is, I was scared to be out. But you already know that, don't you."

I nodded.

"Yeah, well. I've kept up with you through Peter. I don't imagine you've done the same, you know, about me?"

"He's told me some things. I stopped asking after a while. But he's got pictures all over the house."

She smiled. "He loves the girls. He'd have made a great father...."

The text blurred on my can of soda. One minute I was wondering how to pronounce *phenylketonurics,* and the next crying into my very low-sodium diet Coke. Janet had crossed the carpet to where I sat, crushed me to her, and started making all the right soothing noises. And in that soft black place I let go.

I didn't know if I was crying because Peter was dying, because Janet could have had a very different life, or because of my own shattered dreams. All that figured into the equation. I kept seeing Jack, fists dug deep into her pockets, angry and sad at what was being taken from her. As if she sensed that Peter had things to teach her, information her mother didn't possess.

I didn't say any of the things I was thinking. Instead, I let Janet help me out of my pants and under the covers. She slid in beside me, similarly half undressed, and held me as I cried.

A naked Janet straddled me, pushed into me, looked deep into my eyes, and said, "Help me."

"I don't understand."

"Help me."

I didn't know whether to respond to the urgency of her tone or the urgency of her body on mine. I was ready to come. I could see in her eyes that she was too. "Help me," she said again.

I woke myself up when I tried to reach for her face. Opened my eyes to the real Janet, in an old T-shirt, leaning on her side and staring at me.

"You were dreaming," she said. She touched my cheek as if it were the most natural thing in the world for her to do. "You still have the softest skin. I've never forgotten that."

Her touch ignited the desire sparked by my dream.

I recognized the look in her eyes; it held the same urgency as in the dream. The intensity of the days we'd just spent together had stripped that suburban veneer I'd so disdained at first. I'd seen glimpses of the person Janet used to be, the woman I'd fallen in love with. What would happen if I touched her now? Not merely a safe touch on the cheek, as she had done, but an unambiguous move toward sex. My hand on her thigh, between her legs. What if I just pulled her to me? Could I collapse years into this moment? Disregard the past and change the future?

I put my hand on Janet's chest. Her sharp intake of breath encouraged me. I moved my hand down her body. Between her breasts, down her belly. Up and under the T-shirt to retrace the movements. Talk about soft. I eased around to her back, down to cup her ass. I saw her pulse beat in her neck. I felt the charge between us, an echo of the unbridled excitement from years ago. I took hope from her eyes, from the breath catching in her throat. She shifted toward me, as if to hurry my hand. "Please," she said hoarsely, and leaned in close to me.

Time for both of us to tell the truth.

Lips almost touching, no words but maybe we were getting to the truth at last. And to the manifestation of my dream as Janet shifted her weight to swing her leg over my hips.

Then the door between the rooms opened and I heard a whispered, "Mom."

Janet's clear voice answered as she flopped back onto the bed. "What,

Patricia?"

"Can I get in with you?"

I untangled my arm and placed it outside the covers.

Janet scooted toward me. Sheets rustled, the mattress bounced a little.

"I had a dream about Uncle Peter," Patricia said as she settled in. "He was wearing a white suit. He looked very handsome. And he looked like he used to look, you know, before."

I thought of before. Of years of before, when the world was full of possibility, people weren't being swallowed whole, disappeared from the rest of us. I choked on a sob. Janet's hand slid over to me, rested on my hip. Kneaded slowly. What's possible now, I wondered. Hemmed in not just by responsibility but by devastating losses, changes everywhere, my life evolving into something foreign to me, often empty of meaning. Janet's touch spurred my imagination. I could maneuver her hand between my legs, leave her with no question of what and how much I wanted. I remembered her plea for help, heard it as if she'd actually said it to me, not in a dream, but face to face. Moments earlier, her "please" uttered with the same urgency. Once started, where would we finish? I pictured us away from Hollywood, living a normal life, whatever that meant, somewhere small and pretty, just her, me, and the girls.

"Sounds like a nice dream," Janet said.

That startled and confused me for a second, until I realized she was talking to Patricia.

More rustling and shifting of bodies. Patricia peered at me over her mother's shoulder. "Did she spend the night?" She was asking Janet the question, but watching me.

"Yes, she did."

I felt guilty, as if I'd been caught at something. Patricia's look was steady, unflinching, as she stared at me. Even at that young age she had the direct gaze of the lesbian, the woman who can deal straight. I knew what she was looking for, even if she didn't. She held my eye a little longer, then turned away as if deciding something in that instant. Whatever it was, she wasn't sharing with us. She lay back down.

Little feet padded across the room then, and Katy climbed into the bed with us. After some shoving and jostling for position with

Jack, she, too, had a question for her mother.

"Mommy?"

"Yes, Katy?"

"Is Daddy coming here this weekend?"

"Yes, sweetie, he is."

Dreams to dust. In case I needed to be reminded that my fantasy had been just that.

Katy then launched into a detailed account of all the things she planned to show Daddy when he arrived, starting with Uncle Peter's dog and how he swam in the pool.

I fell asleep listening to her words and Janet's encouraging responses.

When I woke, the door between the two rooms was closed, the shower was running, and I was alone in the big bed. The girls had the TV on. Katy was clamoring for a new channel. They fussed at each other, but Jack must have tossed Katy the remote because then there was laughter. Jack was a good kid. Observant, too.

Had she intuited what passed between Janet and me? If not now, she would eventually; she would be able to tell the truth. I thought of her accurate assessment of Peter's dying. I remembered her direct stare. I couldn't transfer it onto her mother's eyes no matter how hard I tried. Janet would never be able to look into another woman's eyes and stay there. My longing throbbed at the thought of being abandoned like that—as if the hurt of years before were happening all over again. How could I have even entertained the notion that she would do anything but return to Seattle with her husband? She wouldn't be back after Peter died, not even to visit. Only Patricia— make that Jack—would come back to Los Angeles. Unlike her mother she'd have no choice but to follow her desire. I recognized that part of myself in her.

The thought made me smile.

DRAGON'S DAUGHTER

cecilia Tan

Memory is a hall of mirrors. When I was twenty years old, I discovered one of the great secrets of the universe: I discovered the magic that ran in my blood and the truth of ancient stories. In one moment, when all of time and space and history cracked open, I knew what my destiny was. But, as I found out, there was still much I had to learn about myself. As I stood on the threshold of the vast timespace that was China, as my power flared to life and I stared into funhouse mirror images of rickshaw drivers and fishsellers and wise *sifus,* I realized at last that I was the Dragon's Daughter. I had come to life from a Chinese fairy tale, but I felt like Alice gone through the looking glass, lost and alone. In that one foolish moment I had lost Jin Jin, and I knew it was my duty to find her again. What I did not know was why I felt so empty. And even as I searched for her in the wide world, anywhere the lucky red sky could touch, I traveled the hall of mirrors of my own memories. I can see myself now, moon-faced girl at piano lessons, dragon girl in silk at the senior prom, stumbling bar hostess with glass dragons hanging from sticks in my hair, placed there so carefully by Jin Jin's hand.

I'm on a street corner in Manila at sunset, the afternoon rain steaming off the hot pavement as the clouds clear the way for that red eye to sink into the bay. It is my second time here, and this time I am prepared. Tea shops that had closed their shutters for afternoon siesta are open now, back-bent people in blue cotton sweeping their stoops and raising their blinds to welcome dinnertime tourists. Neighborhood children spot what they think is a well-dressed man fumbling with his cigarette and begin to swarm around me, selling candies and mangoes, tin birds on sticks made from Coke cans, more cigarettes. They tug on my lapels and I push my way into a restaurant to get rid of them. The proprietor brandishes a broom and they move down the street to intercept others making their way up the hill from the new hotels.

"Can I help you?" he says in Fukienese. He has a Chairman Mao face, balding and basset-houndish. The restaurant is shabby inside, cafeteria-bright with round fluorescents, tiled in chipped white tiles. I doubt Jin Jin is here, but it is the first lead I have. Prostitution is frowned upon, after all, and cannot be asked about too openly. And I must start somewhere.

I clear my throat, tugging at my tie, and quietly inquire in my soft Mandarin about his "house specialty." My suit is impeccable, double-breasted to make my shoulders look broader. I am a milk-fed American girl (though they don't know that) and I tower over everyone in the place. The trick is not hard to pull off. He demurs, in heavily accented Mandarin. I pretend he has misunderstood me and repeat my request, this time putting a hundred dollar bill into his hand. He shakes my hand to return it, saying, "I cannot help you, sir."

"Can you tell me where to go?" I let my shoulders slump. "I've come a long way."

He directs me to a teahouse up the street and off the main drag. That, at least, is something.

When I was fifteen years old, my parents told me I was adopted. It's funny. So many things I remember so clearly: our California living room, the fish tank humming in the silence between my mother's halting admissions, the hunch of my father's shoulders as he sat on the couch, elbows on knees, his slacks riding up his calf and showing his black socks. Like something from a made-for-TV movie. I remember my heart beginning to beat faster and faster under my skin as they talked, while my face stayed stoic, while my surface froze like the ice on a pond. I remember so much, but I don't remember why they chose that moment to tell me.

You came from the mainland, they told me, from the same province as our ancestors. Mom's medical difficulties had led them to the decision to adopt. Mom cried a little while telling me this, and I'm not sure which of us she was crying for. They seemed to think they should have told me a long time before; they had never been sure how to do it. I remember feeling stunned, but it all making sense somehow. I had always felt there was something different about me. I had not known what. That day I thought I knew—I was the ugly duckling in another bird's nest. But how little I knew, how little.

I climb the cobblestone street, stepping onto the crowded sidewalk to let a side-banged Toyota creep past. Watching the crowd, I realize my suit looks too Hong Kong, too upscale, for Manila Chinatown. That's okay, I don't need to pass myself off as a resident. Rich Hong Kong tourist looking for action should be good enough. I pray that Jin Jin is somewhere like here, somewhere small and easy to search, and not Shanghai or Beijing.

I have tested my power since that first accidental visit here. I can go anywhere that is somehow undeniably China. I have been to New York, Los Angeles, Guanzhou, just to look, just to see. I have walked to the past and flown across oceans, all in the blink of an eye. Manila was the first place, though, the first place I stepped through to before I knew what was happening, before I knew not to let go of Jin Jin's hand. She must be here, I insist to myself, but the voice of doubt begins to chant in time with my uphill steps: *It'll take forever to find her. What if you never find her? Never find her, never find her...*

I put the thought out of my mind and swagger into the Red Dragon Teahouse. My heart skips a beat at seeing the name—would Jin Jin choose a place with such a likely name? Would she think to tip me off like that, or would she settle down in the most comfortable place, figuring she might be in for a long wait? Wait for me, Jin Jin, I'm coming.

I take a table in the teahouse and order some dumplings while I examine the surroundings. It's dim inside, with a dark wood interior and landscape paintings on the wall, a much classier place than the previous one. I hope I can afford their house specialty, and have my pick. Then again, this is cash-poor Manila and I have American money. I should be fine.

I had picked up the money from an antique dealer in New York who paid in cash. I'd chosen his shop at random when looking for a place to unload some souvenirs of my experimental trips through the lucky red sky. I'd expected some brusque, suspicious old man and was happy to find Quan young, personable, even friendly.

"Here's four hundred," he had said, putting a pile of bills into my hand. "I'll have another two-fifty for you later." Quan always spoke English with me, a slight hint of British accent betraying either Hong Kong roots or a British education. Whenever a customer would come into his store he would switch to coolie-pidgin: "You like? Fifty dollah." I assumed this increased business somehow, but I never pried. I think I hoped he wouldn't pry back, though of course he always did.

I counted the bills, some crisp, some limp. "How much later?"

"Two, three days. Why, going on a trip?" He leaned on the glass countertop and stuck a ballpoint pen between his ear and his New York Yankees baseball cap. Quan had one of those wrinkle-free, ageless Chinese faces. He could have passed for twenty, or for forty. More like thirty, I guessed. I didn't say anything about where I was going.

"You do a lot of traveling," he pressed.

"Yes. How else do you think I get you all this stuff?" I'd just brought him some jade earrings over two hundred years old. Other than the baseball cap and his cash register, there was little in his shop that looked like it was from the twentieth century, or from this hemisphere.

"Mei, Mei," he said, as if to imply, 'Don't be testy,' but he would never say any such thing. "When do you leave? I'll try to get the money by tomorrow. Meet me for dinner at the Hunan House and I'll have it for you."

Quan wasn't married. He'd told me his father had passed the antique business on to him when he died. I assumed his mother was also dead. He was overeducated for a shopkeeper and fancied himself a historian. Quan tried to get me to have dinner with him on a fairly regular basis.

"Two or three days is fine," I said. "I'll be back."

It is early in the evening and it appears I have succeeded in being the first customer for the Red Dragon's specialty. After I have finished my dumplings and a pot of tea, a nicely dressed middle-aged hostess takes me upstairs, where she seats me in a parlor. We haggle, and I discreetly pass her some cash. Through the thin walls I can hear the sharp twang of women's voices as the whores ready themselves for the night's work. In my mind's eye, I imagine Jin Jin among them, helping them to get dressed, painting their faces. I imagine her leading the group out into the parlor like a madame herself, and catching my eye. I see myself looking like a handsome young man, not like the smoky, drunk businessmen they regularly see. Then, her breath caught in her throat, Jin Jin recognizes me. I choose her, of course, from among all the others, and to her back parlor we go...

My heart is pounding as the hostess pushes aside the curtain and the women come in. I try to look calm. Then I try not to look disappointed. Four women stand in front of me, and it does not matter if they are beautiful or bored, young or old, clean or slovenly. None of them is Jin Jin. I have two choices now: pick one in order to maintain the masquerade, or weasel my way out. I decide to disparage the women, claim they don't look good. The madame assures me these girls are 100 percent Chinese, no Filipino blood in them. The naked racism makes me angry and my stomach churns with bile, but it is a useful lie. I claim not to believe her. I point to this one's nose, the color of this one's skin. I tell the madame to keep the money, I don't care, I'm not letting one of these ape-women touch me. I storm out of the restaurant.

Later, in an alley by myself, I cry.

I had no date for my senior prom. My parents wrung their hands so much over this fact that I kept my mouth shut about what I thought of marriage. I had never planned to get married. Never planned to have children. Somehow I just knew it was not for me, just as I knew I was not going to become an endocrinologist or a surgeon like the two of them, and like they wanted me to. I had learned, though, not to protest too loudly, because if I did, they would moan and cry that if only they hadn't told me I was adopted, surely I would have gone along with their plans. There was no convincing them otherwise. I would just nod and smile and then do what I wanted for myself anyway. So it was when I applied to college in Boston. So it was when I had a relative in San Francisco Chinatown make me a dress. My mother was scandalized that I hadn't picked a more Western dress.

It was imported silk, embossed with tiny flowers, edged with satin pipe, and closed with knotted cloth buttons. It was everything a ballgown should be, a Cinderella dress—a Chinese Cinderella in flat silk slippers. I wore jeans and sneakers to school every day, but for this one night I wanted to be a princess. I think I knew the prom was no place for me, so the only way to do it was to become someone else. Chinese Cinderella danced with all the boys and made all the girls give her funny looks. I didn't find a Prince Charming. I was not surprised.

With the help of a bellboy at my hotel, I uncover more brothels in Manila, and one by one I check them out. The pickings are slim, my insistence on Chinese girls narrowing the search, until I have been to almost every backroom bordello but one. This last is a big one, above a nightclub. In the basement there is a gambling den. The music is loud, which is unfortunate, because if I raise my voice too much it becomes womanish. I keep my sunglasses on and peer over the tops of them as I make my way to the bar. The bartender acknowledges me with a glance. I hold up the business card the bellboy gave me, the name of the place written on the back. The bartender nods and disappears through a mirrored door behind the bar. I take a seat.

People are dancing amid flashing lights and pulsing music. Single men line the bar, some in sharp suits, some holding cigarettes and whiskey in the same hand. None of them even glances at me. I see bar hostesses in short skirts carrying trays through the crowd.

Time passes. A hostess lays her tray on the bar and leans next to me. Her thick, black hair falls in waves down her back. Her lipstick is bright magenta under the bar's lights. She says something in a language I don't know, one of the Filipino languages, I am guessing. I shake my head and hold up my hands.

"You want upstairs?" she says in English then.

I nod. She tugs on my tie then like a dog leash, and I follow her. She skirts the edge of the club and goes up a set of dim back stairs.

On the second floor is a registration desk, as if this had once been a small hotel. A bored-looking Filipino man in a white button-down shirt sits at the desk. He and the hostess exchange a few words. I tuck my sunglasses into the breast pocket of my jacket and try to make it clear what I am looking for.

"Why only Chinee girl?" he asks, with a leer at the hostess.

I put money on the counter in front of him.

"She busy right now. You wait." He jerks his chin toward a vinyl-covered couch across from the desk and takes the money.

I sit. The hostess sits with me, one arm twined in mine. After a few moments, another Filipina comes from down the hall, and snuggles against my other side.

"How long?" I ask the man at the desk, but he ignores me.

The women are starting to breathe in my ears, tickling the small hairs on my neck where I've had it buzzed short. I shake my head as if to dislodge flies. They giggle and begin again.

"Special tonight," one says.

"Two price of one," says the other.

I'm trying to think of the best way to tell them to knock it off, that I want to wait for someone else, when one of them slips her hand onto my crotch. Her eyebrow goes up and I am sure the surprise shows on my own face. This is not a contingency I've planned for.

She says something in rapid-fire Filipino to the hostess, who rubs a hand on my cheek and stands up.

The desk clerk is also standing up now, shouting at me what I can only guess are the local equivalent of *dyke* or *pervert*.

I'm trying to explain myself but there is no explanation for me. One of the girls slaps me across the face. I find myself running down the hallway, opening doors, yelling Jin Jin's name, the man from the desk and the two women close on my heels. But I am the dragon's daughter, and no one can catch me.

I had bought the double-breasted suit in San Francisco, where the tailor seemed unfazed that a woman wanted a man's suit tailored to her. I stood looking at myself in the mirror, resisting the urge to Napoleon my hand between the two wide buttons. I'd gotten my hair cut that morning and it seemed like a stranger, or maybe a long-lost brother, stared back at me from the glass. I had been in San Francisco for a week at that point and was losing hope of finding Jin Jin there. I had been trying to make friends with the whores so I could ask around and see if anyone knew her. But it was difficult to make friends with these women who were, by and large, closely guarded by their men, and who knew very little of the outside world. I could not become one of them, and it took too long to gain their trust. I needed a faster way to go from house to house. It was overhearing the bragging of some Taiwanese businessmen about how many whores they could see in a night that gave me the idea to impersonate them. In the mirror, my twin smiled.

Back in New York, memories of Manila fade like bad dreams. She was not there, not anywhere, and I must decide where to look next. I am in the little pensioners hotel a few blocks from Chinatown proper, where I keep a small place. I am sitting in the kitchen, in the chair with one short leg that came with the apartment. I am waiting five minutes before I try to call Quan again. There is a single phone at the end of the hall that we all share, a bathroom at the other end. I hear the squeals of children through my door and the thump of their feet as they chase one another through the hallway. Quan's phone has been busy all afternoon, and with each try I feel more and more alone.

I should just go down there, I decide. Get dressed and go out. No one here notices me much in the hubbub of families and sweat-shop workers. I wear the same overcoat whether I go out dressed as a man or as a woman, so they can never see. What I'll do when summer comes, I don't know. I suppose there's no real reason to be secretive, or is there? I put on my sneakers to leave for Quan's.

Out on the street it is New York noisy, crowded with people and cars and activity. I chose New York as my hub because it is always easy to find, so similar to the overcrowded beehives of China's cities, cities that have been buzzing for four thousand years. I turn the corner onto the twisted dragon back of Mott Street and then into an alley to Quan's door.

I see him through the window, the shop dark except for the lamp on the counter casting a circle of light onto something he examines with a loupe to his eye. I open the door with a tinkle of bells and his head comes up.

"Mei, Mei! I was wondering when you'd be back. Where were you this time?"

"Manila," I answer, seeing no reason to lie. "It's only been a few weeks."

"Bring me anything good?"

I hold up my empty hands. "That's not what I went there for."

"You have family there?"

"No." I try to give him a look that says drop it.

He bundles up the scrolls he had been examining and makes them disappear behind the counter. "It's late. Do you want to catch some dinner?"

"Quan…"

"Mei, please. I'd just like the company, is all." He shrugs.

I don't have any reason to be afraid of Quan. And I am, undeniably, lonely. "Okay. Let's eat."

When I first met Jin Jin, I thought she was the most beautiful woman I'd ever seen. That is, she *was* the most beautiful woman I had ever seen, and I wasn't even conscious enough of the thought to know I had thought it. It was only later when I began to realize what my thoughts were, as she occupied more and more space in my head. My poor overworked brain, crammed with women's studies classes and contradictory politics and comparative literature. When I arrived at the restaurant to begin my evening's work I would forget it all.

Jin Jin's hands were soft as they brushed my hair and pinned it into place, as they buttoned my silk embroidered bar hostess dress.

Each night she transformed me from an overworked college student into something more elegant. But she herself never changed.

Quan steers me to a table at the restaurant, near the kitchen door. I want to protest, but it does not seem to be worth the effort and he appears slightly nervous about something. I sincerely hope he is not going to ask me to marry him, a worry I only become conscious of as we sit across from each other. Quan pours tea for the two of us. We each sit sniffing the jasmine steam in silence. He sits with his back to the wall, a garish painting of some folk scene hanging above his head: it's a parade of villagers led by a man carrying two buckets of fish on a pole hung across his shoulders. I smile at the memory of Jin Jin telling me the story of the fishseller who became immortal by accident. If I ever see her again, what stories will I have to trade?

Quan sees me looking at the painting and says, "Do you know the story?"

"You mean about the Immortal Fishseller?"

"He wasn't immortal while he was a fishseller," Quan says. "He used the pill of immortality to keep his fish fresh. But when the other fishsellers tried to steal it from him—"

"I know, I know, he hid it in his mouth and swallowed it."

"Thus becoming immortal, but no longer being able to sell fresh fish."

"I wonder what he did after that?" I put down my tea. "Are there other stories about him? Stories end, but they are never really finished, are they?"

Quan peers over the top of his cup at me. "He decided to travel and see the world. But he always wound up coming home again. If he spent too long away, he found his mortality slipping back, bit by bit. Whenever he returned, though, the seven lucky gods smiled on him."

I feel my eyes narrow as I look at Quan. "Cute." I am still imagining that he's either going to hit on me or propose, and am trying to anticipate where what he says is going to lead. So I am completely unprepared for what comes next.

He puts down his cup and says, "I know who you are."

"Like hell you do," I say, annoyed for some reason I cannot define.

"I know the stories, too," he says, and I can see his face reflected brown and round in his tea cup. Like the man in the moon.

"Mei, listen to me. I'm not the only immortal in China. I know another one when I see one. And you..."

"I'm not immortal." I want to tell him he's crazy, but it feels wrong. What would Chinese Cinderella say? "I was raised in the States. I had a childhood, a life."

He shrugs, matter-of-fact. "There are three kinds of immortals, Mei. You, you can die and be reborn. Me, I've lived one long life." He closes his mouth as a waiter puts plates of bright vegetables down in front of us. A bowl of steaming rice clouds the air. "That doesn't change who you are or what you can do."

My heart hammers, and I'm not sure why I have the urge to run from the room. I feel my face beginning to freeze; I blink my eyes rapidly. "What do you want from me?"

He makes a disgusted noise. "I don't want anything from you, Mei. I wanted you to know about me. I wanted you to know that we can help each other. I can introduce you to some others, if you want. Even Wong F—"

I grab his hand. "Do you know where I can find Jin Jin?"

He cocks his head; he does not know that name.

"The emperor's concubine."

His mouth opens in a silent *oh* and he nods. "I have not seen her for a long, long time."

"I'm looking for her," I say, not sure that I can explain why. "She, she's waiting for me."

"Mei—"

"How can you tell who the other immortals are? Is that why you helped me when I first came to you?" The food sits, uneaten, in dishes between us. "Can you help me find her?"

He starts scooping rice onto my plate, then his own. "One thing at a time. Yes, I knew you were someone right away, I just was not sure who. Once you began to bring me things, well, it could only be you. I'm not sure how to help you find her."

"But how do you recognize the others?"

He begins to eat, chopsticks clicking against the plate. "Center yourself and relax, and see how the world looks. Some things will seem thin and insubstantial, things that won't last. Others will seem vivid and solid. Buildings, people, roads. Some of them are part of us, some are not."

"I've never noticed that."

He shrugs. "What can I tell you, that's the way it is. Either you see it, or you don't. What have you been doing thus far to look for her?"

I describe my incognito investigations.

"Needle in a haystack," is what he says to that. He shakes his head, sadly. "And what will you do once you find her?"

"Take her back, I suppose. Wherever she wants. Whenever she wants."

"And then?"

I stare into my plate of rice and vegetables.

"Mei," he says, his chopsticks still for a moment, "you do know who she is, don't you?"

"What do you mean?"

"You know the story—she who was so loyal to him that the gods granted her immortality. She's looking for her emperor."

"Of course she is," I say, annoyed, but for some reason on the edge of tears. I start to eat, angrily grabbing at the food with my chopsticks, chewing hard.

Quan eats quietly for a while, politely looking away while I calm myself. Then he goes on. "I said there were three kinds of immortals."

"Yes. Like me, like you, and…?"

"And like Jin Jin. Mei, she's lived one long life, like me, but she is not like me. She is…the embodiment of an ideal. Perfect loyalty. The woman behind the throne. The yin that yang power demands to balance it."

"That sounds like a warning."

"She's…she's not like you."

"What are you saying?" I am ready to jump down his throat if he criticizes me or tries to tell me any more about myself that I don't already know. I am angry at him for forcing me to see what I already knew: she does not feel for me the way I feel for her. "She's not like what?"

"She's not a person, she's an archetype. She is perfect, and cannot change. That's why she wants to go back, because there's no place for her here, now."

We eat in silence as I digest everything he has said.

When he speaks again, it is with a soft, forgive-me voice. "Have you looked in New York yet?"

"No." I am calmer now, but still a bit taciturn.

"Perhaps I could make some inquiries by word of mouth." His desire to help seems genuine.

"Thank you." I feel I should apologize for being angry with him, but now is not the time or place for that.

He goes on. "And have you considered that she might be in Boston?"

I stare at him.

"When you lost her, you were in Boston, isn't that what you said? And the next moment you were halfway around the world, in Manila. How do you know she went anywhere at all?"

I cannot chew because my heart is in my throat.

"You never went back to check?"

"I was afraid to." Skinny Dou and his army of cooks waiting for me. I'd tried to steal his golden goose. But, god, what if she had gone back? "Quan, you must help me."

He opens his mouth to speak, but I overrun him with a sudden plea, my anger and reserve gone. "Come back with me to Boston. They don't know you there. They'll recognize me, but you, they don't know. And you'll be able to tell if it is her. All you have to do is go into the restaurant and order the house specialty. Then tell me if she's there." How could I be so stupid? I am suddenly certain she is there. "We can go right away. I'll have you back in an hour."

Quan sighs. "I suppose I have nothing better to do."

I almost kissed a girl once when I was fifteen. She was thirteen, but very sophisticated in a feminine way, her red hair curled, her nails painted. She had just moved into the house across the street and was due to start at my school in September. Our mothers conspired that we should socialize together. I followed her around like a puppy. I loved the way she smelled, the way her hair curled, her white skin like a porcelain doll. Before her first date with a boyfriend, she decided she needed kissing practice. So in her bedroom, all hung with pictures of unicorns and horses, she asked me to pretend to be her boyfriend. I agreed. But then we went on talking as usual, and we never kissed. I wondered if I was supposed to interrupt her, sweep her off her feet or what. I thought she'd stop at some point and say, okay, let's try it. But she never did, and we never mentioned it again.

I am standing on a Boston street corner at sunrise, looking up at the reflected sky in a plate glass second-floor window. Quan is back in New York with a gift from me of two more jade earrings over a thousand years old. The back streets are quiet, the steel grates down over shop doors, the waterfall sound of rush hour coming over the tops of the buildings. I make my way to the back of the building, where the kitchen door is propped open. Amid the clang of woks and the hiss of frying and running water, I hear Skinny Dou's voice. He is yelling at one of the kitchen workers, which one I cannot guess. He is busy, that is all that matters to me.

I open the door to step through, but it is not the kitchen I enter. With a shift of the universe, I emerge in Jin Jin's room.

I find her at the window, looking out at the sunset, her hair unbound in her lap and the comb idle in one hand. She crosses the room to me, a tiny smile wrinkles her eyes. I take her hands in mine.

"I'm sorry," I find myself saying. "I didn't know."

She nods.

"I'll take you where you want, when you want. You don't have to wait anymore."

She nods again. I am in a hurry to get us away, but she stops me with a few quick words in Mandarin, her voice sweet and high like a bird by a stream. She wants to be ready.

From a wooden chest she unearths a silk dress that covers her from throat to ankle. I help her to button it over her shoulder and down her back. Then she sits in front of the mirror and I take the black silk of her hair in my hands. There are so many things I want to know, and yet I cannot bring myself to squander these moments with chatter. My hands and hers move together over her hair, binding it up with two slender lacquered sticks.

When I had first come to work for Skinny Dou, I had an idea in the back of my mind that I could fool people into thinking I was something I was not. My mother was ashamed of the "restaurant" side of the family, and had raised me to be as American as apple pie. But when I was fifteen and I learned I had come from the mainland, I began to undo that any way I could. I tried to teach myself to read Chinese and failed. When I went to college I tried again and succeeded, but I had thought it too late—it was too late to be who I had been meant to be. When I took the Chinese restaurant job, it was one more stab at grabbing a piece of the life I felt I had missed. But fate takes care of these things, and upstairs in Skinny Dou's restaurant, I found a true piece of the past waiting for me like a piece of jade buried in a box of silk.

I center myself and take a deep breath. All around us the hall of mirrors glitters, as if we stand at the center of a mammoth diamond, every facet the entry to another world. "Look," I say. "Look." Like waltz partners, we turn in a slow circle, the facets blossoming all around. A kaleidoscope.

Then her breath catches in her throat and she pulls me onto a street of packed earth. We huddle against a high wall as she cranes her neck around one corner. I crouch and peek also, into a shrine, where a young man is making his obeisance to his ancestors. Around him candles flicker and incense burns but he seems to glow with a luminescence of his own. Jin Jin covers her mouth and pulls back, one hand against her chest.

"Thank you," she tells me, "thank you."

"Is this good-bye?" I can barely speak. It feels as if a giant hand is squeezing my throat and my chest.

She leans forward, one crystalline tear in her eye, and brushes her silken lips against mine. Then she rounds the corner and is gone.

My heart is a hall of mirrors. I stand at the center of being, at the center of everything, and look into the future, the present, and the past. I belong everywhere and nowhere, and know not where to go. One step and my destiny will be decided. I float between worlds and consider. There is no folktale in which the dragon's daughter dies of a broken heart. Stories end, but they are never finished. I go in search of a lucky red sky to call my own.

HUEVOS RANCHEROS

carla trujillo

Wham! Something hit the bed.

"Marci, wake up!" Corín said, pounding the bed again. "You're talking in your sleep."

"I was?" I looked around but couldn't see very good.

"Yeah, a lot."

I rubbed my eyes.

"You were laughing, too. Must've been good."

"It was."

I was sad. It felt so real. Everything was like it really happened—the letters, knives, tying Eddie up, even cutting him. I rubbed my eyes some more, then looked around the room. I wondered if we would have killed him. I clenched my hand into a fist, then slowly opened it. I guess I'll never know.

I sat up and looked out the window. It was light outside. The sky was pink. I don't know why it was that color, but when I went outside to water my corn, which was now as tall as me with stalks as fat as my wrist, I looked at the sky and was amazed it could be so pink.

Maybe it had something to do with the fact that we lived close to Union Oil, or maybe it was because everybody was burning trash that day. I always thought the real reason was because my Grandma Flor and Tío Alfonso drove up to the house that morning in their Cadillac convertible. I couldn't believe my eyes. There she was, sitting with Tío Alfonso right next to her. Grandma Flor owned the car but always made Tío drive it. She said she was a princesa and that was just the way it was.

Grandma Flor had a red scarf over her head. Her hair sticking out the sides was purple black like an eggplant. She had on cat's-eye sunglasses and red lipstick to match the scarf. She was the only person I knew who had millions of lipsticks to go with anything she wore. She was smoking a cigarette and slowly getting out of the car. Grandma Flor was not little. She was about five seven and had no fat on her. Her skin was brown and wrinkled, and the muscles on her arms and legs were hard.

Tío Alfonso was moving kind of slow, too—from driving, I guess. His skin was really dark, and he had thick, black hair. He said he was from Gallup, but Eddie said he was really from Louisiana and that he wasn't an Indian like he said he was, but Colored, trying to pass. I didn't believe Eddie because he didn't like Tío Alfonso, so he could have made anything up. Tío Fonso, which is what me and Corín called him, made Eddie mad because he thought Tío was just a no-good freeloader who lived off my grandma.

Grandma owns a corner bar, so she isn't rich, but she used to have these old shacks that she rented out to people. When the city wanted to build a new courthouse exactly where they were, they had to, as Grandma put it, "pay the price." That's how she got the Cadillac and that's how she met Tío Fonso: he sold it to her. My mom likes Tío Fonso, even though she says he's a little young for my grandma.

I was surprised and happy to see Grandma Flor. She lives in Gallup, and as far as I know, has always lived there. I think about her a lot and wish I could see her more than I get to. She's smart, and good at bingo, too. I call her the seeing eye dog of bingo players. She's so good she can look at ten bingo cards, keep her eyes on my and Corín's cards, and still have time to talk to her friends. She smokes without stopping from the second she gets up 'til she turns off the light at night. When she talks, the cigarette hangs out the corner of her mouth. I don't even know how she sees with the smoke from the cigarette climbing like a snake into her eyes.

Grandma plays bingo, but she's no kitten. She stabbed Grandpa Carney, who was my mom's dad. His real name is Encarnación. We saw him maybe two or three times, but he never remembered who we were. He drank a lot, and my mom said she guessed Grandma got sick of it 'cause they got into a fight and Grandpa was beating her when she pulled a knife off the kitchen counter and stabbed him in the stomach. Twice. The police came and took Grandma to jail but let her go when she told them what Grandpa did to her. Everybody in Gallup knows Grandma because of her bar. Grandpa Carney lived. Some said it was because of his name. Other people said it was because he was too mean to die. But he sure didn't come around anymore after that. When he took off with that gabacha who used to come in to buy a six-pack of Pearl beer every Friday, Grandma said good riddance.

I ran up to Grandma to hug her. She raised the arm with the cigarette high over my head so it wouldn't burn me, gave me a kiss on the lips, and hugged me tight.

"Mira, look at you, look how big you are!" she yelled loud enough for practically the whole neighborhood to hear.

"Hi, Grandma!" I yelled back. "I didn't know you were coming. Hi, Tío."

Tío Fonso came around and shook my hand.

"Hello, good morning," he said, like I was a princesa too. He's always nice to me. He never talks very much. Mostly he smokes cigarettes, drinks beer, and watches all-star wrestling.

"Qué estás haciendo? What are you doing? Where is you mama y tú daddy?" Grandma asked fast and loud.

"Eddie is in the back doing something, I don't know what. Mom's inside." I looked at her proud. I knew she'd think it was funny I called Dad Eddie.

Grandma took a puff off her cigarette and looked at me hard for a second. I saw her eyes squint up in the smoke like she was about to laugh, but the only sound that came out of her was *hmmph*.

Corín must of heard them drive up because she ran out of the house straight into my grandma's arms.

"Grandma Flor! Hi, Grandma!"

"Mira, y tú tambien. You're both getting so big."

She hugged and kissed Corín, then held her out so she could look at her close. I saw her eyes go all over my sister, then they stopped at the scars and bruises on her legs. She looked over at my legs.

"Por qué están so flacas? How come you guys are so skinny, eh?" she asked, then smiled real big. "Did you say hello a tú tío?"

"Hi, Tío Fonso," Corín said softly, then slowly reached up to shake the hand he held out to her.

"Hello, Corín. How are you?"

Tío Fonso looked tired, like he wanted a beer.

"Come in everybody," I said, like I was the boss of my house. "Did you drive all the way from Gallup?" I asked, but they didn't answer because my mom walked out with Eddie right behind her. Tío Fonso walked around the car and opened the trunk to take out the suitcases. I went to help, but Eddie beat me to it. They shook hands.

"Quehúbole! Cómo estás?" Eddie said to Tío Alfonso, shaking his hand hard, then each of them grabbed a suitcase.

"Hi, Mom, I didn't know you were coming." My mom looked a little surprised.

"Hi, mija," Grandma said as she hugged my mom. "Cómo estás?"

"Fine, fine."

"Well, I'll be goddamn! Talk about a surprise," Eddie said.

"Hello, Eddie," Grandma said, hardly looking at him.

She stood smoking with her hand on her hip and talked to us like she was giving a speech. "Pues, estamos a un drive en mi new carro, so I said, 'The hell with it, Fonsito, let's go to California and visit my mijítas.' So here we are." She reached down and hugged me and Corín.

I thought it was weird that she never told us she was coming, but I didn't say anything.

"Entre, entre. Come on in," Eddie said back to my grandma. "You guys must be muy cansados."

They walked into the house and sat on the couch.

"Sí, poquito, pero I'm just happy to see Marcía and Corín. Come over here and give your grandma another hug."

We went over to her and hugged her again.

"Rosa, get me a beer and get them something to drink. Flora, qué quieres?" he said to my grandma.

"Café, nada mas."

"Y tú, Alfonso, café or cerveza?"

"Café, gracias."

Mom got up to get them their drinks and I followed her into the kitchen.

"How come Grandma's here?" I whispered.

"No sé," she said back, real fast.

"She never comes without telling us," I said as I opened the fridge to get the beer.

"Just get your dad a beer."

I got the beer and the canned milk and Mom followed with two cups of coffee. I could tell Eddie was trying to do all the talking, but Grandma wouldn't let him. She talked fast, and then when he tried to talk, she wouldn't even wait for him to finish his sentence. Tío Fonso was already in front of the TV watching Roller Derby, and Eddie and Grandma had moved into the dining room. I wanted to watch Roller Derby too because I liked Big Anis Jensen, who played for the Bay Area Bombers, but I was more interested in what my grandma was saying.

Grandma sipped her coffee with a really loud slurp. She untied her scarf and her pressed-down hair puffed up like a thick black sponge. She lit another cigarette. Lucky Strike was her brand.

"Well, I no gonna beat around the bush," she said as she took a deep puff off her Lucky. "I come here to take Rosa and the girls with me to Gallup for a vacation." She blew out a bunch of smoke into Eddie's face when she said this. "A long one."

"A que cabrón." Eddie's face wrinkled up into a frown. "Now just hold on there, lady. Who the hell says you can come over here and do what you want with my wife and kids?"

"No te digo nada, except this is my daughter and my grandchildren and I gonna take them to my place for a little while." Grandma said this with the cigarette hanging from the corner of her mouth.

I don't think they saw me and Corín watching and listening to everything. I looked over at Corín. Her eyes were giant. Eddie looked over at Mom.

"Rosa, did you have something to do with your mom coming out here?" Eddie turned to her and practically yelled it in her ear.

She sniffed loud but wouldn't look him in the eye.

"I thought so." He said it like it made him sick.

"La Rosa no dije nada a mí. She just say she was tired. The girls are on vacation, so I told her come visit your mama." She kept talking with the cigarette hanging out of her mouth. When she finished, she took a long puff and let the smoke out with a hard breath of air. I thought Eddie's head was going to explode. His face had turned red and his eyes looked like slits of lava.

"I want to go with Grandma," Corín piped in.

"Me too," I said.

"You kids stay out of this. This is none of your damn business. Me and your grandma here's talking. Better yet, go over into the living room and watch TV with your tío." Eddie tried to flick us out of the room like flies. We didn't move.

"I said go!" he yelled, and looked at us with those eyes that could melt steel. We knew that look and got up to leave.

"Déjalos. Let them stay." Grandma said it soft but strong. We sat back down. Then, as if nothing happened, Eddie seemed to forget we were there.

"Mira, Flora, this is *my* family. You can't just come here out of the blue in your fancy car, pick them up, and drive away. This is my wife, and these are my kids. Mine! Not yours. Mine!" His voice was loud and he was pounding the table with his pointer finger.

I looked over at Mom. She had one leg that kept bouncing up and down and held both of her hands together like she was praying. She didn't look at anybody, just down at the table. Her hands were pressed together so hard that the whites in her fingernails showed.

Tío Fonso quietly walked into the kitchen and got himself a beer. He didn't go back to the TV though, he just stood in the doorway, watching.

Grandma Flor picked another cigarette out of her silver cigarette case and snapped it shut. She shoved the cigarette in her mouth and lit it with her lighter so fast you almost thought it lit itself. She took another long puff and looked at Eddie like she could easily kill him.

"Mira, let me tell you something." She pointed her finger. "Your wife and kids are not your slaves. You married my daughter and you helped bring these kids to this earth, but I got some news for you. You don't own them."

That was all it took: Eddie went for her. He tried to choke her, but before his hands got a good grip on her neck, Grandma pulled a switchblade from her pocket and laid the tip under his chin.

"Ay Dios!" my mom gasped.

"Sit down, cabrón! And take your goddamn hands off my neck!" Grandma looked like she would gladly use the knife. Eddie slowly let go of Grandma Flor's neck. His hands didn't know what to do so they stayed in the same place, only now they were just in front of him. He looked down at them, saw what they were doing, and dropped them to his sides.

"Eddie, why don't you sit down like the lady asked you to?" Tío Fonso had quietly walked up behind him and spoke right in his ear. Eddie looked shocked. His eyes, still hot, flitted all over the room, first to Grandma, then Mom, then me and Corín, and finally back to Tío Fonso. He slowly sat down in his seat.

Grandma laid the knife on the table, but kept her hand on top of it. With the other she smoked her cigarette. She looked right into Eddie's eyes. Except for the puffs from Grandma's cigarette, the room was totally quiet.

Finally, Eddie looked away.

"Chingáo, man. I guess you wear the goddamn balls in this family, que no?" he said like he was kind of laughing.

"Mira, I don't wear the balls, but I got enough of them to stand up to you. Leave these kids alone and treat your wife for once like she ain't your dog."

"Nobody!! Nobody!"—he pounded the side of his hand into the table like he was karate-chopping it—"tells Eddie Cruz what to do! Not my wife, not my kids, and especially, not you." With that, he pushed himself away from the table.

"Eddie—"

My mom tried to grab him by the arm, but he shook it off and walked out of the house, slamming the door behind him. We heard the car start, then the wheels scream as he drove away.

Mom ran into the living room and looked out the window like she wanted him back. I first thought this was going to be the luckiest day of my life until she turned around and I saw how much she was crying. Something told me right then that we weren't going anywhere. Mom wasn't going to leave Eddie no matter what he did to her, or how he was to us. And, as if she read my mind, Grandma whispered to Tío, "She's never gonna leave him."

I looked for Corín and saw that she had sunk down into a corner, crying. Something about seeing her and my mom cry made me feel like I weighed a thousand pounds. Like I was sinking into the tar of the La Brea Pits. I knew then that even though I wanted to leave, I couldn't. Not by myself. I couldn't leave Corín and I know she wouldn't leave without Mom. When I looked at Grandma, I felt what I needed to do. When I looked at Corín, I felt the same thing—but opposite.

Grandma put out her cigarette.

"Bueno. You girls want to go with your Tío Fonso and me, or are you staying here with your mama?" She asked the question matter-of-fact, like how I wanted my eggs cooked.

I thought about it for another second, then looked over at Corín.

"I can't go without my mom, Grandma," Corín said, crying harder.

"Y tú?" Grandma looked over at me.

I slowly shook my head.

"Bueno. Vamos, Fonsito." She started gathering up her things. She took the switchblade, folded it up, and put it in her pocket.

"No quieres lonche?" My mom walked into the kitchen, her eyes watery, and started getting things out of the fridge. I could tell she was trying to act like nothing happened.

"No, gracias, mija. It's better if we go."

Grandma and Tío walked to the living room. They picked up their suitcases and walked out the door. While Tío loaded the suitcases back into the car, Grandma hugged all three of us.

"You be good," she said to Corín as she bent down to hug her. "And start eating a little more. You look too flaca."

Corín smiled.

"Y tú también." She hugged me hard and gave me a kiss on the lips. "You and Corín are gonna fly away with the wind." She stopped to puff on her cigarette. "Mira, tóma. I almost forgot. I bring some presents for you two." She looked inside her big purse and brought out a present for me and one for Corín.

"Thanks, Grandma," said Corín. "Can we open it now?"

"No, no. Wait till I go."

Both of them were in skinny boxes about six inches long.

Grandma pinched my cheek and looked over at Mom. She turned back to me. "You help your mama," she said, her eyes diving deep into mine.

"I will," I said, and started crying. Then she hugged me again, hard.

When she finished hugging me she turned to my mom and put her arm around her. "I no gonna tell you to leave him. He's your husband. But I want you to know that you and the kids can come and stay with me anytime. I mean it, Rosa, anytime. Entiendes?" Then she stopped, stared at Mom, and put both hands on her shoulders. "Rosa, don't be like me—I waited too long." With that she turned and got in the car. She took her scarf out of her purse, tied it over her hair, and lit another cigarette.

Tío Fonso came over and shook our hands. "Adiós," was all he said.

Grandma didn't look at us anymore. She stared straight ahead as Tío started the car and gave it some gas.

"Bye, Grandma!" yelled Corín, her eyes filling up with water.

"Bye, Grandma," I yelled too.

"Bye-bye, mijítas," Grandma said, turning around to take one last look at us as Tío Fonso put the car in gear and drove away.

"Thanks, Mom!" my mom yelled loud, louder than anything I ever heard come out of her.

Grandma had already turned back around. She was almost out of sight when she lifted her hand up and waved like she was in a parade. She was still waving as the car sped around the corner.

While no one was looking, I opened my present. I lifted the lid off the box and there, against black cardboard, was a flicker of turquoise and silver. My very own knife.

SKINNER AND CHOY

KITTY TSUI

'm in trouble."

    I kept punching the rewind button to replay the tape.

    "…it's Skinner and I'm in trouble."

    Zzzzzzzzzz…

    "Hey, Choy…"

Maddening.

"Hey, Choy…it's Skinner and I'm in trouble."

I felt like a jilted lover still obsessed with the voice of her beloved.

"Hey, Choy…"

Or perhaps I fancied myself a PI…

"…it's Skinner…"

…searching for clues…

"…and…"

…in the background noise…

"…I'm in trouble."

…the proximity of foghorns. The cacophony of bells at a railroad crossing. A cablecar rounding the street corner. But there was nothing but the soft susurrus of the tape and the loud thumping of my heart.

Finally I pushed the answering machine away with a fury that sent it skidding across the glass tabletop, and threw myself onto the sofa. Feeling a tension headache threatening to begin, I closed my eyes and covered them with my fists.

Alison Skinner. I grew up in England and she had been my childhood best friend. She showed me how to make a mean catapult and shoot bull's-eyes. She had been a patient teacher until I mastered a bike without training wheels. It took a while. The dread of balancing on two wheels was akin to my horrific fear of heights.

When my grandmother who lived in San Francisco sent me a skateboard, I had been Alison's teacher; we had become the envy of everyone at school. No one else had a skateboard from America. Alison Skinner was bossy and loud. She loved to play practical jokes on the unsuspecting. I was shy, quiet, and bookish. Even physically we were at opposite ends of the spectrum. She was taller than I, had a chunky body and thick legs. I was skinny, bespectacled, and bowlegged. We were an unlikely pair, but we became fast friends.

We began drifting apart during the last year of high school. Alison began to skip classes for days at a time after her mother died suddenly and in a mysterious way. At first I kept calling, stopping by her house. But she was morose and unapproachable. Then she ran out of her house brandishing an iron poker. Her eyes afire with rage, she had screamed at me, "Bloody Chink! I am not your friend. Leave me alone."

I had not seen her again.

I had my own problems. I was to sit for the O-level examinations at the end of that school term. And my family was making preparations to emigrate to America. She and I had no further contact. On the airplane across the Atlantic coming to the States, I wrote her a ten-page letter. It was an emotional one, filled with anger and sarcastic barbs. But, of course, I had not sent it, and writing to her was the last time she occupied my conscious mind. I wiped Alison Skinner from my memory, like rubbing an eraser across penciled doodles on a sheet of foolscap.

I lay on the sofa trying to ease the throbbing in my head. The strange thing was that out of the blue, I had been thinking about her that day. Even stranger, riding the streetcar home, I had glanced up at a missing persons poster. Though the face was not the face of the child I remembered, it had been her name. Alison Skinner. Alison spelled the English way.

I had repressed that memory of her shaking a poker and shouting obscenities at me, preferring to remember only the more pleasant times we shared. There had been many. We belonged to a tomboy gang of two, her and I. And we called our gang Skinner and Choy. We frequently got into scrapes of one sort or another, but we always managed to get out of them. Sometimes she rescued me; other times I rescued her.

I thought back to one Guy Fawkes Night long ago. What happened that night had, without a doubt, jelled our friendship.

It was a beautiful autumn day and the first time in weeks that the sun had appeared. Alison and I took our usual long way home, a circuitous route through the Breck, sprawling acres of a no man's land where tangled underbrush grew unchecked, and rusted tin cans and paper trash proliferated like wildflowers. Dressed in our incongruous school uniforms of brown gabardine blazers, white shirts, and tunics with pleated skirts (we did, however, wear knee-high socks and sturdy oxfords), we clambered over boulders and swung from low-hanging tree boughs, laughing and carefree. We chattered about everything. From discussing the recent adventures of Hergé's cartoon character, Tintin, the boy reporter, and his dog Snowy, to chanting our favorite poems.

Hers was William Blake's "The Tyger":

"Tyger! Tyger! burning bright
In the forests of the night..."

Mine was "Kubla Khan" by Samuel Taylor Coleridge. In an exaggerated, solemn voice, I would begin:

"In Xanadu did Kubla Khan
a stately pleasure-dome decree...
I would build that dome in air,
That sunny dome! those caves of ice!
And all who heard should see them there,

And all should cry,"
And Alison and I would shout in unison:
"...Beware! Beware!
His flashing eyes, his floating hair!"
Then she would, with great mocking effort, dance around and mime:
...Weave a circle round him thrice,
And close your eyes with holy dread,
For he on honey-dew hath fed,
And drunk the milk of Paradise.
And we would both burst into gales of laughter.

We reached a clearing ringed intermittently with fallen tree trunks where the night's festivities would take place. Guy Fawkes had been a Roman Catholic soldier involved in a conspiracy to blow up the House of Lords on the opening day of Parliament on November 5, 1609. The plot was foiled and Guy Fawkes hanged for treason. In celebration, ever since then, the citizenry built bonfires to burn effigies of Guy Fawkes. In present times the festivities include bonfires and fireworks.

At the Breck, a huge pile of wood was collected, twigs and dead branches augmented with splintered planks from broken packing crates. A motley crew of boys hung about, the older ones smoking cigarettes and directing the younger ones to do the work of dismantling the crates and removing nails from the wood.

Peter Horner, the class bully, saw us and scowled, "Wha' ya lookin' at, eh? Go on wi' ya! Yer bloomin' knickers smell!"

Alison and I both stuck out our tongues at him and ran, laughing, out of the clearing, then separated, each to our own home. We would eat a hurried supper, change clothes, and meet up again for the fun at the Breck at nightfall.

Alison and I both loved Guy Fawkes Night. Like most of the town kids, we were allowed to stay out later than usual and unchaperoned. This always elicited from us our happy battle cry which we screamed in unison, "Yipppeeeee!"

My dad was away at sea. He was the First Mate on board the Pyrenees, a Blue Funnel liner that carried half cargo and half passengers. For ages I had been baffled by what "at see" was. My laconic mum didn't bother to explain, and it was Alison who had finally helped me out.

"You dope," she exclaimed. "Cripes, she means he's at *sea,* not at *see!*"

"Oh, I see," I answered, terse as my mum. Thanks to my pal, the light had come on at last.

Mum and I had our usual supper. Toast with butter spread thinly with Marmite, tinned pilchards swimming in tomato sauce, and strong tea. For dessert mum had made jam tarts, my favorite, filled with strawberry jam.

After I did the dishes, I was about to run out the front door when my mum called out in Chinese, "Did you wrap up good? Take your scarf and mittens."

"Yes, got 'em," I lied in English. "G'-bye."

I grabbed my blue-and-brown striped woolen scarf but left my mittens on the shelf in the hall closet. I detested mittens; they were for kids. Alison never wore them. She was a hardy one. She'd live with chilblains on every finger before she would tolerate mittens on her hands. So would I.

Alison and I usually met at the intersection of Bluebell Avenue and Dorset Lane, but we had decided to rendezvous at the site of the big bonfire and watch out for each other there.

With the imminent approach of winter, it had already been dark for some time. A large crowd gathered around the bonfire. Children played with sparklers, and there was the smell of wood smoke and roasted chestnuts in the night air. A group of boys roughhoused near me. Suddenly, I was jostled. I turned, hoping not to encounter Peter Horner and his pals, but they were not boys I recognized. One of them glowered at me. I ignored him and stuck my tongue out at him in my mind's eye.

I walked on the outer edge of the crowd, scanning the faces, aglow by the light of the flames, but I could not find Alison anywhere. I was surprised. It wasn't like her to be absent on Guy Fawkes Night.

I took a sweet from my pocket, unwrapped a cube of toffee, and sucked on it, savoring its taste in my mouth. A young couple with a toddler wrapped in a blanket gathered their bag and turned to leave, so I drew closer to the bonfire and its welcome warmth.

I finished the sweet and was about to reach into my pocket for another when a gust of wind hit me, striking me like a slap on the face. It so startled me that I had to keep from crying out loud. It was as if an arrow had pierced my body. Fear shot through me. I broke from the crowd and ran helter-skelter through the undergrowth. In the dark, branches lashed out at my face; rocks and roots grabbed at my feet. A dog howled in the distance. Something big and black flew at me—was it a bat, or a plastic sack blowing in the wind?—and I tripped and hit the ground. I lay where I fell, panting, my heart thudding in my chest. There was no moon, and the night was pitch black except for a mosaic of stars. I found the North Star, Orion's Belt, and the Big Dipper. And I waited for my heart to calm down.

"Cripes!" I said aloud, in a braver voice than I felt. I was determined to brush myself off and walk home, blaming Alison for my plight. She could jolly well fend for herself, I thought, wherever she was.

It was then I heard laughter. Jeers. A scream.

"Alison?" Her name sprang from my lips.

I got to my feet and looked around me. Behind was the glow of the big bonfire and up ahead, to one side of a clearing, I discerned a faint flickering of flames. I approached cautiously. Cigarette smoke mingled with the smell of burning wood, beer, and charred bangers. By the light of a campfire, I could see someone tied to the trunk of a tree, their backside a flash of white buttocks striped with ugly red welts. Peter Horner held a strip of something in a gloved hand and he was applying it with force to the naked bum. Four other boys ringed the scene, laughing, passing around a bottle.

I froze. Then, without thinking, without a plan of action, I burst into the clearing, waving my arms like a windmill. Words like stones erupted from my mouth. "Scram, you beasts, scram! The bobbies are coming. Scram. Hey, here," I screamed, "they're over here. Hurry, hurry. Don't let them get away."

I lunged at Peter Horner, who raised his hand to shield himself from me. The thing he had been holding whipped across my face with a red-hot sting that burned a trail across my cheeks.

"Help, bobbies. Hey, over here. Here!"

I heard my friend shouting too, both our voices proclaiming unholy vengeance.

"We're here. It's Peter Horner and his gang. Get them!"

The boys ran as if their trousers were on fire. I got up, went to my friend and cut her from her restraints with my penknife. She pulled up her knickers and her slacks, rearranging herself with a quiet dignity. Her face was streaked with dirt and wet with tears, but her eyes were as bright as fire.

"Where are they?" she said, her eyes questioning.

"Who?" I asked blankly. "Peter Horner?"

"No, the bobbies."

"Oh, the bobbies...I made it up," I replied.

"You what? You balmy or something?" Alison said in an incredulous voice. "They could have got you too!"

Then she started laughing so hard she sank to the ground.

"You are daft, Choy."

"What is so funny? I just...did it."

"Oh, my bum hurts," she moaned, between her laughter. "That sod must have hit me with a bunch of nettles."

"Serves you right," I said. "Next time I will go get the police and let you suffer longer."

"Oh, oh," she howled. "'Help, bobbies, over here. Here!'"

"Glad you're having a fun night after all. Here," I said, handing her a sweet. "Shut your gob and have a piece of treacle."

I fingered my face. Raised flesh where Peter Horner had struck me with his nettle whip flamed and itched.

The night sky burst into light as Roman candles and rockets signaled the beginning of the fireworks display.

Alison and I, both of us dirty and disheveled and laughing like maniacs, walked out of the Breck arm in arm, physically linked for the first time. We didn't say anything. We didn't have to.

I was exhausted. It was Friday night and it had been a long week. I am the chief fundraising officer for a large AIDS service organization. I had completed a major grant proposal, done two presentations for corporate sponsorships, and finished an annual report for the upcoming board of trustees meeting. Whether in meetings or on the phone, I work with people all day long, and I had been looking forward to doing absolutely nothing on the weekend. Now Alison Skinner's cryptic phone call hung over my head like the sword of Damocles.

Dammit, I thought, uncharitably. Why did this person from my childhood suddenly surface? It's been years. I probably wouldn't know her if I bumped into her on the street.

Used to be I'd crack open a beer or uncork a bottle of wine after work. Now that I'm clean and sober, I've had to reprogram myself. I walked the four blocks down to my gym in the Castro, where there are almost as many gyms as there are bars per square block. I biked hard for forty-five minutes. When I returned home, I made a cup of roasted barley and brown rice tea and climbed into bed with a paperback.

Within ten minutes, I was asleep.

It is gray and overcast. I am walking in thick fog and can see nothing. The roar of the ocean thunders in my ears. It is a strangely soothing sound. I am walking toward a golden light that shines in through a break in the white bank of fog. I walk into the light and am enveloped in warmth. A woman approaches me. She looks somewhat familiar, but I cannot immediately place her. She is naked, but neither her nudity nor my own surprises me. She is taller than I am, and her hair falls loosely about her shoulders. The light casts a gold sheen on our bodies. I want to touch her. She smiles at me, and I reach out for her as she reaches for me. We embrace in a timeless moment. Joy infuses my being. I want to hold her close to me forever.

Suddenly a preternatural sound snaps into my consciousness. The call of a bird? The clanging of temple bells?

The telephone roused me from my dream. I debated whether to answer or let the machine pick up, but the insistent ringing would not cease. I remembered I had turned off the machine when I listened to Alison's message earlier.

"Yes?" I snapped into the receiver.

"Choy, it's Skinner," came a voice.

"Alison Skinner? Unbelievable. Where are you? What's going on?"

"Are you alone?"

"Yeah, I'm alone. Why?"

"I can't talk on the phone now. Listen, I've got to get off the line. Where are you? Can I come over?"

"Uh, yeah. Hey, what's going on? What kind of trouble are you in anyway?"

"Uh, later. Just tell me where you are."

I gave her directions and went to take a shower. I had a feeling it was going to be a long night.

I waited almost two hours before she showed up. By then I was sure I had imagined the whole thing. When the knock finally sounded, I immediately tensed, unsure of what to expect. I went slowly to the door. Opening it, I faced the woman in my dream. I stared at her, my mouth agape in surprise.

"Hey," she said. "You going to let us in or what?"

"Huh? Us?"

She rolled her eyes at me.

"Haven't changed much, hav' ya, luv? Laconic as ever, eh?"

It was then that I noticed a dark mutt sitting quietly at her feet.

"Come in. Sorry, I was caught by surprise."

"What, mate? Never met a dog before?"

"Very funny. I haven't seen you in what, twentysome-odd years and you drop in on me like this. Yeah, I'm surprised."

"Well, how do you do and all that. This here is Skipper. Just call us Skinner and Skipper. And Choy," she added with a grin.

That was a look I remembered. A lopsided grin that bared her slightly crooked side teeth. But gone was the chunky body and the oily hair and thick bangs that hung over her eyes.

"Want coffee or something?"

"How about a drink? I need one."

"Sorry. I don't have any alcohol in the house."

"Oh God, don't tell me you're one of those clean and sober fanatics."

"Well, I am clean and sober, but no fanatic. I've got Coke and juice, coffee or tea. Your choice."

"Coffee'll be okay. And how about some water for Skipper?"

"Sure. Come on, pal."

The dog followed me obediently.

"What is he, some kind of hound?" I called from the kitchen.

"He's a she, and she's a German short-haired pointer."

"Oh, sorry. Where'd you get her?"

"She's an orphan. I adopted her from the humane society a while ago."

I brought back the coffee in mugs. Skipper followed at my heels.

"Sugar or milk?"

"Nah, black's fine."

The dark dog went to Alison, licked her hand and whined.

"No, baby," she crooned. "Stay on the floor."

Skipper whined again, then turned a beseeching gaze on me.

"What?" I asked.

"She doesn't like floors," Alison said, a sheepish look on her face. Now it was my turn to roll my eyes.

"Oh, go ahead. It's fine, she can sit on the sofa with you."

"Thanks," she grinned. "Come on, girl, up."

The dog skipped up on to the sofa and arranged herself, mostly on Alison's lap.

"So," I said, sitting across from her. "I can't believe it. What are you doing here in San Francisco? In my house? I haven't seen you since we were kids. And what's more, today on the streetcar I saw this missing persons poster with the name Alison Skinner. I didn't really recognize the photo as you, but the name attracted my attention."

"It's a long story…"

"Why am I not surprised."

"No, really. It is a long story and may sound like a fib, but it's true."

"Okay. Try me."

"The missing persons poster, it's a ploy."

"Ploy? What are you talking about?"

She drank her coffee, clutching the mug in both hands.

"I'm not missing, I'm running."

I threw up my hands in the air. "You're running? I'm lost. Would you just cut the shit and fill me in. Don't tell me you're running from the cops."

"It's worse."

"Oh no, I'm not sure I want to hear any more."

"You've gotta help me."

I hit my forehead with one hand and shook my head. "You're in trouble, aren't you? What kind of trouble?"

"Look…okay, I'll tell you straight. My downstairs neighbor is a drug dealer…and…uh…"

"Oh, shit."

"I've been hanging out at his place, and we're, well…friends."

"Uh-huh," I moaned, wondering where this was all going to lead.

"No, it's not what you think."

"I'm not thinking anything yet. Why don't you just fill in the blanks."

"We are just friends…I'm gay," she yelled.

"Whatever," I yelled back.

Skipper jumped.

"Skittish thing," I commented.

"It's not her fault. She was abused. You should have seen her when I first got her, poor little thing."

"Okay, why don't you go on with your story. I think I can handle it. You're gay, you and he are friends, you're doing drugs with him, is that it. Okay, so what?"

"Do you want to tell the story or shall I?"

"Okay, you tell it then."

She took a deep breath. "He went to New York for three weeks and asked me to take over the business for him while he was gone. He gave me explicit instructions about everything. How much to cut…"

"Cut? Oh, no! You're dealing coke, aren't you?"

The look on her face told me the answer. Before I could say anything, she pressed on.

"I thought he meant that I could keep the profits, just sell and buy for him."

"And?"

"I gave him his money," she burst out.

I was getting agitated. "So, and?"

Skipper looked up and whimpered.

"Don't shout. She gets upset."

"She's upset? It's my house and I'm upset!"

Skipper jumped off the sofa and came to me, her tail between her legs. I petted her silky fur. In seconds, her stubby tail was wagging a mile a minute.

"Okay, girl. I'm mad at your mother, not you."

"Choy, calm down, it's not that bad."

"I'll be the judge of that," I grunted.

"Uh, I took off with a quarter ounce of Peruvian flake."

"You what—oh shit. This can't be happening to me," I said, shaking my head. "I have a druggie in my house who's in possession of a quarter ounce of cocaine and she's running from a coke dealer. Do I have that right?"

"Well, I'm not a druggie."

"Oh, you're not? What are you? You do coke, right? What else are you on? Do you have that quarter ounce on you?"

She nodded her head. "But it's not like I'm addicted or anything. I mean, I don't do it all the time. Look, I haven't had a line for hours."

"And you won't be doing any lines in this house."

"Okay, okay. You gotta help me, Choy. I don't know what to do."

"Oh, shit, shit, shit," I repeated.

I got up to brew another pot of coffee. Alison and I talked until the dawn light brightened the night sky. Skipper had been snoring on the sofa for hours, oblivious to our conversation. I made Alison give me the baggie of cream-colored Peruvian flake. I held it in the palm of my hand. For an instant I recalled what it felt like to take a hit, that electric rush, the numbness in the gums, the bitterness in the back of the throat. Then I wondered how much it was worth, cut and on the street.

"We'd better get some sleep," I finally said. "I don't have a guest room but I've got a big bed. Unless you want to curl up with Skipper on the couch."

"I'll be fine out here with Skipper," she began. "Anyway, you probably don't want to have a lesbian in your bed."

"There is a lesbian in my bed," I deadpanned.

She looked at me and grinned. "Well, in that case, Skipper and I will come join you. We'll figure out what to do tomorrow."

"We?" I cried. "You've got a bloody nerve."

"And you've got your bloody Liverpudlian accent back. Thought you'd dropped it."

"You've got a bloody nerve," I repeated, laughing. "But, yeah, tomorrow's another day." I draped my arm over her shoulder. "You know, something's been bothering me for years…about that day you came at me with a poker."

"Yeah, I suppose I do need to give you an explanation. Me mum died. It was silly, really, a needless accident. You know my dad drank and I hated him. Wanted to play a trick on him. He used to hide bottles all over the house. One day I went around and took all of them. He kept his main stash in the basement. I loosened one of the boards on the stairs. Figured he'd fall, knock himself out, and mum and me'd be rid of him for a coupla hours. The old bugger sent me mum down to fetch one for him. She slipped. Broke her neck. It was my fault, really, but of course I never told anyone." Alison began to shake and I put my arms around her.

"Shhh, you don't have to go on."

"No, I've kept it inside all these years. I've got to finish this now. I hated myself. When I came at you with the poker it was because you were the closest person to me. I loathed myself. I couldn't tell you, and yet I couldn't keep it a secret from you. Anyway, I figured I didn't deserve to have a friend like you. So I chased you off."

"Oh, Alison."

I pulled her down next to me on the sofa and held her as she cried.

Thoughts roiled in my mind, spiraling like images in a kaleidoscope, disjointed fragments of light and color. I could not foresee what lay ahead for her and I certainly had no idea how I was going to help. But I did know I was glad she had called me. She was safe in my home for the moment. Tomorrow she and I would sit down and try to sort things out. One step at a time. I looked up and saw a framed silk-screened poster in my hallway, a colorful rendering of three words: *Keep It Simple.*

I held her close to me and kissed her cheek, tasting the saltiness of her tears. "Come on," I said gently, "we're both exhausted. Let's deal with everything tomorrow."

"Yeah," she sighed. "Okay."

I pulled her up. She put her arm over mine and we walked to the bedroom together, physically linked once again.

"Tomorrow…," she said.

"Yeah, tomorrow. Tomorrow, there's always tomorrow…" I sang.

"It's only a day away," she joined in.

We grinned at each other and finished the song together. It was like we were kids again with no time or space between us.

"Come on, Pumpkin," Alison called over her shoulder. "Hey, girl, let's go."

The dog jumped off the sofa and followed us to bed.

TO THE FLAMES

JESS WELLS

ENGLAND, 1486

t's not actually that difficult to kill a bishop. They're slow-moving and gullible. Fond of eating, they are prone to illness and poison, especially when they have women serving them in the parsonage and women hanging by their necks in the square as witches.

Bishops are easy to stalk, and as I am a shape-shifter, I can follow them like smoke through an alley. I am a woman in a man in a woman, depending on the cloak and the breeze in from the sea.

I was going north, following the flight of the medicine women across Europe, heading to Ireland to save their lives, north in stealth across the short protective sea, deep into the isolation of the Celtic people. The women medical students from my mother's university scurried through towns with satchels, shawls over their heads as they ran from the burnings, holding medicines and one of my manuscripts of the medical teachings of Trotula under their wraps.

The thick books were millstones around my legs as I crossed Europe with my mule and my cart, carrying out my mother's orders to deliver one hundred copies of the writings of Trotula to women doctors and hospitals throughout the Continent. Sometimes I would separate myself from the mule, since I could shift but my mule was always the same. The black cat I befriended could get us in almost as much trouble as the manuscripts, as they are the first sign of a witch. Little kitty learned to love living inside her burlap bag. I left them both on the outskirts of this village and ventured near, skittish, uncertain that I was any longer capable of human contact.

You see, I had killed my first cleric only days ago, and I had heard his blood pour out onto the flagstones of his church. It had howled like wind, leaving me to search for a way to stop my incessant pacing, the screaming rage inside me that had started when the cleric's head hit the flagstones with a thud. I was growing a new skin and not certain what kind of animal it would make me. But my task was clear. I circled this village, having an inkling that a bishop was planning this as his next destination.

I had been sent to find Elizabeth Brentwood, not a medic but a supporter, and as my life had evolved into a series of clandestine jumps from the shadows of one woman's life to another, from the safety of one supporter to another, Brentwood's village was a welcome sight. I watched her from the behind her hay bales.

Elizabeth Brentwood's stride, as she paced from her stables to the storage shed, was so large that the children running behind her couldn't jump from footprint to footprint. Her body parts seemed to defy containment: her breasts heaved and swayed inside the corset and her gauzelike modesty panel; her legs threatened to gobble up the ground until they shredded the skirt that covered them; hands hauled things that required two men; arms ripped the seams from her dresses; and her mouth spewed language that would land a man in a brawl. She was a big woman, not particularly tall but twice as wide as a man. Her jet black hair was so thick, it couldn't be tamed with pins or hats, and she wasn't a woman for ribbons. No, she was not that sort at all. She wove her hair with cowhide thongs and lanced it to her head as if it were an unruly piece of luggage strapped to one of her wagons. Everything about her warned you to stay back and watch the fireworks. I followed her movements, hidden only a few paces away.

The sun was already bright and hot by mid-morning. I observed as Elizabeth turned to the rain barrel, flung off the heavy lid with one hand, and dowsed the front of her chest. A thin, dusty driver walked up close beside her and muttered under his breath. Elizabeth looked startled, then grabbed the reins of his horse and drew the animal up to her. The driver continued to speak beneath his breath as Elizabeth forced open the lips of the gelding.

"Don't look so frightened," she growled, half at the horse, half at the driver.

"It's different this time," the driver said. "They's the big guys."

"A couple of broken-down priests," she dismissed.

"No. There's scores of 'em, riding in line with their banners and their cloaks. And the bishop's not the biggest, ma'am. He rides to the left of a very fancy man. University fella on the right of him. Could tell from his cap. But I can't imagine who would be so powerful to ride in the center with the bishop, but he does. And I'm tellin' ya, Elizabeth, they're headin' right this way."

"Who's the man in the middle?" she asked, confused.

Sprenger, I wanted to howl from my hidden post. Jakob Sprenger, my nemesis. I had begun to see his book on the lab tables and in the cleric's offices as I maneuvered among the clergy, trying to deliver medical knowledge to women doctors and unloose a few women from their grip. The Hammer of Witches, *he called it, his textbook for torturing women and fabricating confessions. Rid the world of Sprenger, rid the world of pain I was convinced. This was the village where wrong would be righted. Vengeance would be mine. The other cleric had simply been practice.*

"How long?" Elizabeth said, surreptitiously inspecting the horse's ears.

"By this evenin', I'm sure."

"This evening! That's not enough time. You're supposed to send a rider ahead!"

"The wagon broke down and I lost my lead," he whispered. "I had to go the way 'round to get ahead of them again."

She pushed the horse aside with a violent thrust.

"How many times have I told you!" she shouted at the driver. "You rotate the horses on the return trip. Left to right. Now take this animal up to the top pasture and then you bloody well walk the way back!"

The driver mounted, and Elizabeth struck the rump of the animal so hard the horse shot out of the village.

Of what are women capable when bartering for their lives? Willing to be walled up in convents for the simple chance to read? Become a shape-shifter and a murderer to save bedraggled midwives and a manuscript of herbal potions? Alison Peirson of Byrehill, a gifted healer, cured the Archbishop of St. Andrews of an illness the physicians couldn't fathom, yet he refused her payment and executed her for witchcraft. I was there, and I say she missed a glorious opportunity to rid the world of another man who would go on to kill legions of women. This time, I had arrived ahead of the murderous convoy, and Elizabeth Brentwood, though not a healer, though not an entire school of women, was worthy of saving.

"I can help you," I whispered to her as she stood, unmoveable, in the dusty crossroads of her self-made world.

She whirled around, missing the sight of me entirely. "Who's there?"

"I can help you with the bishop."

"Show yourself," she growled.

I stepped forward, but not entirely out of the shadows. It was a netherworld I had grown to consider home.

"Beggar, out of my village."

I dropped my hood and she saw my close-cropped raven hair, my eyes. Had my recent killing made me grow scales on my skin, horns or protrusions, as I felt it had? Brentwood didn't turn away.

"I can rid us of the bishop…and of the man in the middle," I said.

"Who are you?"

"Kore, a disciple of Trotula the healer. Sent across Europe as a protector of her word."

Elizabeth furtively looked around her, then regarded me with ferocious eyes. It was too much to ask a woman to trust me immediately, but time was short.

"Harm comes to the bishop, I will most certainly die," she whispered menacingly. "No. It has gone too far for that. And they've come too close. I control everything south of the river bend and they know it."

She stepped away from me. "Beggar! Out of my village," she shouted, then turned and charged away.

I had no choice but to fade into fog, cross the fields, and follow Sprenger's entourage. I had tracked him for nearly a month now, though with a life like mine one can never be certain of time. I followed them into the village, into the boardinghouse, where the three men held hankies over their noses and insisted that the tables and chairs be scrubbed before they sat. Oh, to have been a three-headed spear at that moment, to pierce them once and for all.

I crouched in front of the fire, a servant, feigning to sweep up the ashes. I had seen university professors scurrying into the midwives' houses after the women were hauled away to burn. The professors confiscated journals, vials, herbs—anything to teach them the medicine they were too lazy to learn on their own. Bishops picked out the wealthiest women to fill the Church coffers, the loveliest women to rape.

But Sprenger was here, within a leap of me. Did I have a blade long enough? No, I would have to let him cross the room. While the other two muttered about sanitation, Sprenger strode through the room in a fancy cape and a tight red headdress, pulling back the curtains with his riding crop. Sprenger. I had never been this close to him, and it made me tremble. I took inventory of my knives and potions deep in the folds of my clothing. I felt light-headed trying to formulate a plan.

He crossed the room with a huff and plopped himself like a petulant child into a large chair right in front of the fire. His putrid boots were stretched out right beside my nose as I scrubbed.

Just then a small man scurried into the boardinghouse. I must say that at first, from the corner of my eye, I thought it was a possum scuttling in as he moved about, bent over and sniveling. The alderman, he sheepishly explained, offering up a ledger. Tax records. Who paid what, who owned what. Women in possession of land. The alderman perspired heavily and tried to rub the mud off his worn boots onto the back of his pants leg. His thinning hair was arranged to cover the scabs on his scalp. Bowing and scraping, he begged pardon, made obsequious gestures, darted around the room.

"Elizabeth Brentwood," the bishop asked the alderman, looking up from the ledger. "She is the wealthiest woman in the village, isn't she?"

Elizabeth Brentwood, the grit in his wound. The alderman owned the blacksmith shop and his business depended on her, but she blocked him. There was no way for him to expand because she was always launching another caravan of wagons into London before he had even thought up the plan. Taking on new horses, hiring her own blacksmith. She was haughty. A shrew.

"She takes part in the Maypole celebration?" the bishop asked.

"Well," the alderman stammered, "the whole town does. It's just a Spring celebration…"

"The entire town?" Sprenger stood sharply and leaned across the table toward the alderman. "Is there enough wood nearby to take the whole town up?" he said gleefully, screwing his face into a sinew. "The whole town? It's been so long. Come along, Bishop, let's take the whole place down." Sprenger turned toward the curtains in a pout. "Brian, brother Brian, let's burn up quite a few here, shall we?"

The bishop stood between Sprenger and the alderman, his hands behind him as if to try, in some way, to calm Sprenger down.

"Of course not the entire town, just…most of the women," the alderman blustered, spittle jumping onto his lips and falling into a scraggly goatee that was clearly more of a food trap than an adornment. What would it be like to see Elizabeth Brentwood go up in flames? A cold sweat gathered on his forehead. He thought about her money filling the village coffers after she died. The bishop had his back to him; the alderman bit his lip to keep from smiling.

"You're an idiot," the university professor growled in the alderman's ear, as Jakob Sprenger started to dance on his toes through the room.

"I beg your pardon, sir?" the alderman whispered.

"If you kill her, the Church takes her money. If you marry her, you take it. Given the choice…"

"And have you ever heard her speak of the Devil?" the bishop said without turning back to the alderman.

"Yes, the Devil!" Sprenger chortled. "These are evil lives, these witches. A social pest and parasite, a devotee of a powerful and loathsome—"

"Now calm yourself, Jakob," the bishop warned.

The professor continued to mumble in the alderman's ear, alternately slurping from a goblet of dark wine, his teeth purpled.

"But if you implicate her and then marry her, you're as likely to go on the pyre as she," the professor said. "They're very thorough like that. You'd become the faggot, the kindling to set the blaze."

Sprenger jumped to his feet, strode to the far end of the room. He threw his cape over his shoulders and proclaimed, "A loathsome obscene creed. Remember the Book of Revelations: 'The great whore that sitteth upon many waters with whom the Kings of the earth have committed fornication—'" He stopped abruptly, spun around, and stuck out an accusatory finger at the alderman then continued, "'I saw the woman drunken with the blood of the saints and with the blood of the martyrs—'"

"Oh, not Brentwood," the alderman quickly interjected. "Contributes heavily to the Church. Nothing of the witch in her, no indeed," he said nervously. He twisted the end of his shirt in his fingers to hide the dark lines of dirt under his nails.

"'And I,'" Sprenger pronounced with a sharp finger in the air, "'shall make her desolate and naked and shall eat her flesh—'"

"Sprenger!" the bishop barked sharply, ordering him to silence.

"'—and burn her with fire. And in her,'" Sprenger went on, laying himself across a table, "'I found the blood of prophets and of saints and of all, that were slain upon the earth.'"

"Get our fine orator and leader a mug of wine, young man," the bishop said to me, kicking me with his boot. "The point is, alderman," the bishop continued, commanding the room once again, "what about Brentwood? Brentwood's not a witch, you say?" The bishop turned. "Not the fat one with the stables?"

"I dare say there isn't a soul in town who has anything on her," the alderman stammered, bowing and twisting as he approached the bishop. "Give me another few days and I'll see what I can do to find...the real witches."

"Yes, yes," said Sprenger, circling back toward the timorous man, "you find me some witches. Do that, alderman. Find me some."

The wind tore down the dark lanes of the village, howling against the stone walls as the alderman pulled his hat down and his cloak around him and scurried toward Elizabeth Brentwood's house. She lived at the end of the lane, as far from her own stables as she could get, she said. He had to rap several times on the door before her maid answered. He squirmed inside and without seeing me dart into the shadows, forced the maid to close the door behind him. Elizabeth was sitting at a desk, working on her daily reports.

"Simon," she said with disgust and surprise.

"They've come for you," he said breathlessly, breaking his hat in his twisting palms.

The maid gasped, stepped back a few paces from Elizabeth, then pulled her cloak off a peg. "I'm sorry, ma'am," she muttered, then flung open the door and ran out of the house.

Elizabeth, startled from her chair, began to protest the maid's departure, but thought better of it. If they had come for her, they would surely string up her servants as well.

"The bishop is here, and Sprenger himself. They'll have you for witchcraft. They will," the alderman said, leaning on the table, "for consorting with the Devil."

"I consort with no one," she growled. "Now get out of my house."

"As much evidence as they need. A woman without a man? Surely a witch."

Elizabeth glowered at him. Things had certainly gotten worse. The stories coming in from her drivers raised the hair on her neck. Previously, they had been only occasional tales, told when they thought she couldn't hear, but now the men arrived pale and frightened, sometimes sitting in the hayloft with their faces in their hands before they could address her. If Sprenger himself was in town, they would be looking for big fish to fry, and she was the biggest fish in these parts.

"They'll have you strung up in the catacombs before the week's end," the alderman continued. "There's only one way out."

"I've paid my way out of this kind of mess before, alderman, and you know it, so don't tell me there's only one way."

"Marry me," he blurted.

Incensed, Elizabeth charged across the room and pushed the alderman so hard he landed against the far wall of her house. She outweighed him by two hundred pounds. She stood more than four inches above him and with fury in her eye, he barely dared to collect himself from the floor.

"Marry me," he said again, timidly, curling himself into a little ball. "They have only one charge against you, and that's that you're not married."

"You've been scheming for my money for years, you sniveling goat's ass!"

"Better to have half of your estate than no estate, no future, no life," the alderman pleaded.

She spit into the fire at the thought of such a man. But he was right, Elizabeth knew. "Marry you?" she shrieked. She couldn't stall any longer. She had been paying off the priests who came in to town, but this Sprenger wouldn't take no for an answer.

Elizabeth picked up a chair and heaved it behind the alderman's head, smashing it against the wall. She strode toward the alderman so violently that the house shook, then grabbed him by the collar and pulled him to standing. A filthy, witless, disgusting little man. And he was her ticket to life.

"You want to marry me?" she growled and hauled him with one hand onto her desk. She held him down with one massive hand on his throat and pulled apart his threadbare pants with the other. He whimpered as she pulled his cock out and roughly made him hard.

"I'll show you marriage," she said, hauling her girth onto the desk. She mounted him, with a sneer on her lips and tears in her eyes. She scooped him up like a rag doll and pounded him into her.

"You're mine now, little man, and if you betray me," she said, tearing a swatch from his pants and holding it as evidence, "I'll see that they burn you beneath my skirts!"

I slipped out of her house when she threw the alderman into the mud of the street. She grabbed her cloak, hauled him out of the dirt with one hand, and dragged him to the abbey on the outskirts of town to be married. With Sprenger already in the village, there was no time for betrothals.

I paced the wagon ruts outside her door. If the bishop died, they would round up all the women and throw them to the flames. If Sprenger were murdered, the whole town would go up. If anything happened to any of them, Brentwood would die. I had come so close, and yet now I had to let them slip through my fingers. Sprenger had been near enough to me that I could have slit the artery on his thigh before anyone would have known that I had turned. I had lost my chance, had made myself ineffectual. He distributed his manuscripts of death; I distributed mine of health. But he was winning, educating a generation of clerics on torture and extermination. And my people had given up hope to flee north.

I wasn't able to kill Jakob Sprenger or the bishop that time, and my path moved from stalker to journeyman. There would be other encounters with Sprenger and his book of death, because this is a story of survival, of slow triumph at great cost.

Over the years, Elizabeth gave birth to twelve children with the alderman. Eight of them lived—daughters who rode with me across Europe delivering manuscripts. We confined ourselves to the hospitals that had been established by the dynasty of women healers born to Eleanor of Aquitaine, wife of Louis VII of France and later of Henry II of England. Her daughter Isobel founded the Poor Clares, who transformed their nunneries into hospitals. Isobel's granddaughter Hedwig, Queen of Silesia, Poland, and Slavic Croatia, built more than eighteen thousand asylums for lepers. Blance of Castille, granddaughter of Eleanor of Aquitaine, built a gothic hospital twenty-five miles from Paris, and her daughter, Isobel, Queen of Sicily, built a hospital near Dijon, both of which are still standing. St. Elizabeth of Hungary, niece of Hedwig, and one of the finest healers of all time… well, another instance of arriving too late to help.

On through Europe we traveled, soon with Elizabeth's grandchildren, who took for granted that I never aged, watching the Black Plague and the Inquisition turn the countryside into a morgue. Watching the fear mount until even Paracelsus, considered one of the great scientists of the Renaissance, buckled under their pressure in 1527. I begged him to let me carry his book with that of Trotula, but he burned his entire text on pharmaceuticals because he had made it no secret that he had learned it all from the medicine women. He avoided the flames, but the knowledge did not. Bad choice, I told him with an angry grip on his collar, and we never spoke again.

HUNGARY, 1605

If truth be told, even a woman with a potion for longevity from her mother gets weary, and in 1605 I couldn't bear it any longer. I had scurried through the worst of the witch-burnings in England and Scotland that began in 1590 and were to continue until 1650. By then they had established special "burning courts." In 1605 I met Margarita Fuss, Mother Greta as she was called, since people find mothers so much less threatening than women doctors. The daughter of a birth attendant to the nobility, she was forced to earn her living after her husband proved incapable of organizing his finances. She studied medicine with her mother and then went to Strasbourg and Cologne for more education. While they burned in England and Scotland, she traveled all over Germany, Holland, and Denmark delivering babies.

I'll never forget meeting her in a clearing one morning when I was despondent over my task. She was dressed in a red-and-black striped skirt, a jacket like that of a Hungarian hussar, carrying a bag with a snake emblem embroidered on it. She was leaning on a gold-headed cane.

I must have looked like a forest peasant, half fairy half leaf, but she wasn't startled when I approached her, which is rare. I am such a shape-shifter that I can walk face front for twenty paces toward someone and still not be seen. But I had noticed her bag. I had sensed a compatriot, and in my fatigue I could not put up defenses. I held out the manuscript as if reaching my hand up to be pulled from over the side of a cliff. She said one word to me.

"Trotula!" She was surprised. Impressed.

"Carry it," I whispered, as if I would crumble when the sentence ended.

And, in fact, I suppose I must have because I remember her laying me into the leaves. I remember darkness and then flames, hot broth, the sight of her striped skirt, her pointed black shoes, the book open on her lap. I remember dappled sunshine and her sending away gawkers who hovered nearby. When I finally cleared my head, she took me by the arm and insisted I sit before I stand.

"How old are you?" she asked me.

"I have no idea," I lied.

"What is in that vial on your chest?

"I don't know."

"Where are your people?" she asked.

"Burning in the town square."

She looked away, adjusted her cane, began again.

"Where are you from originally?"

"The medical university of Solerno."

She nodded, then smiled. She picked up my hand. To this day, I can feel her hands on my body like the hands of my mother on my face. Mother Greta raised my hand to her lips and kissed me. "I have heard of you," she said quietly. "I thank you for your work."

Well, let me tell you that if I had a heart that hadn't already been burned out of me, I would have wept to the end of my days. I would have. As it was I staggered under her grip as she pulled me to my feet.

"You remind me of the Italian. Ancient beyond her body's years. They say she was a professor. She's in Ireland with the rest of them, and it is full of flames from here to there, so you must go now. Get across England to Ireland and rest."

Mother, I thought. Could it be my mother 177 years later? She had given me the vial—surely she would have kept one for herself. Wouldn't she have wanted to be with me enough to wait? My task was done, wasn't it? Couldn't I possibly rest and go where a woman's hands would cup either side of my cheeks and bring me home, tell me that whatever shape or smoke or flame there had been, I was her daughter, that we were one? Mother Greta stopped a passing wagon with a wave of her hand and put me on it, bound for a quiet life with my mother, in Ireland.

Time is such an odd thing. I had always thought it fast in joy and slow in pain. But the boat trip across the channel was too fast: it sped me toward a place where my last hope of my mother might be cold peat, a bag of bones, a wooden headstone. Surely she was alive, I whispered to myself, ready to believe what my head knew couldn't be true. I was 189 years old I had calculated on the boat; she would be beyond all measurable time. I couldn't bear to walk the last miles to her house couldn't bear to raise my hand to her door. To lose something you want, to finally give up all hope—the food your heart has gnawed on for these many years—well, the loss of the hope is sometimes a greater pain than the joy could ever be when the desire was finally gained.

I tried to turn back, but I arrived, knocked with my face drawn and my weariness unable to shield me from any blade or noose or truth the building would unleash. The door opened on a very lovely young woman who surveyed me, then blanched at the sight of the vial around my neck. "Madam!" she called out behind her and opened the door. "Madam, it's true!"

My mother sat on a bench by the fire, huddled under blankets. She dropped her cup of tea at the sight of me, made sounds like a forest animal and opened her blankets, her shawl, pulling them around us as I joined her. I have had no understanding of time, seeing women born, grow, wither, die in what feels like a bird's life span, but when my mother put her hands on my cheeks, when she held my face, then stroked the vial as if thanking it for being a watchdog she had commanded to stay by me, I felt all the days without her pressing in, all the years of longing for her breaking my shoulders.

"They are delivered," I said to her in my old woman's voice, with my old woman's lips, crumpling into her arms.

"Then we are safe," she whispered, pulling my cheek against her butter-soft face, and turning us to regard the flames.

ABOUT THE AUTHORS

LUCY JANE BLEDSOE is the author of the novel *Working Parts*, winner of the 1998 American Library Association Gay/Lesbian/Bisexual Award and of *Sweat: Stories And A Novella* (both from Seal Press), and of two novels for young people, *Tracks In The Snow* and *The Big Bike Race* (both from Holiday House). She is the editor of *Gay Travels: A Literary Companion* and *Lesbian Travels: A Literary Companion*. Her work has appeared in the *Advocate*, *Curve*, *Girlfriends*, *Fiction International*, *New York Newsday*, and *Ms. Magazine*.

NISA DONNELLY is the author of *The Bar Stories: A Novel After All*, which won a Lambda Literary Award for Lesbian Fiction, and *The Love Songs Of Phoenix Bay* (both from St. Martin's), and the editor of *Mom: An Anthology Of Lesbians Writing About Their Mothers*. She lives in California.

JEWELLE GOMEZ is the author of four books: a collection of short fiction, *Don't Explain; Forty-Three Septembers* (essays); a novel, *The*

Gilda Stories, winner of two Lambda Literary Awards (Fiction and Science Fiction); and *Oral Tradition: Selected Poems, Old & New* (all from Firebrand). Her work has been frequently anthologized in both academic and trade titles. She is the Executive Director of the Poetry Center and American Poetry Archives at San Francisco State University.

JUDITH KATZ is the author of two novels, *Running Fiercely Toward A High Thin Sound,* which won a Lambda Literary Award for Lesbian Fiction, and *The Escape Artist* (both from Firebrand). Her work appears in *Tasting Life Twice, The Penguin Book Of Women's Humor, Hot & Bothered, Friday The Rabbi Wore Lace,* and many other anthologies. She teaches at Hamline University, the University of Minnesota, and Minneapolis College of Art and Design.

RANDYE LORDON is the author of the Sydney Sloane mystery series, which includes *Brotherly Love, Sister's Keeper, Father Forgive Me* (winner of a Lambda Literary Award), *Mother May I?,* and *Say Uncle.*

LINDA NELSON is a writer and freelance editor who moonlights as Vice President of Technical Services for a New York City-based consulting firm.

ELISABETH NONAS is the author of three novels, *For Keeps, A Room Full Of Women,* and *Staying Home* (all from Naiad), and co-author with Simon LeVay of the nonfiction *City Of Friends: A Portrait Of The Gay And Lesbian Community In America* (MIT Press). After eighteen years in Los Angeles, she now lives in Ithaca, New York, where she teaches screenwriting at Ithaca College.

CECILIA TAN is the author of *Black Feathers: Erotic Dreams* (HarperCollins) and *The Velderet* (Circlet Press). Her short fiction has appeared in numerous anthologies including *Queer View Mirror, Dark Angels, On A Bed Of Rice, Hot & Bothered,* and *Best Lesbian Erotica 1996 and 1998.* She and her cats live in Cambridge, Massachusetts.

CARLA TRUJILLO is the editor of *Chicana Lesbians: The Girls Our Mothers Warned Us About* (Third Woman Press), winner of a Lambda Literary Award (Lesbian Anthology) and the Out/Write Vanguard Award for Best Pioneering Contribution to the Field of Gay/Lesbian Lifestyle Literature. She is the editor of *Living Chicana Theory,* and the author of various articles on identity, sexuality, and higher education. She works as an administrator in diversity education and advocacy at the University of California, Berkeley.

KITTY TSUI is the author of *Breathless* (Firebrand), winner of a Firecracker Alternative Book—FAB—Award in the sex category, and *Sparks Fly* (writing as Eric Norton). Widely anthologized and widely photographed, she lives in the heart of the Midwest with her two dogs, Meggie Too, a Hungarian vizla, and Hershey, a German short-haired pointer. Hershey is thrilled to be the model for Skipper in "Skinner and Choy."

JESS WELLS' ten volumes of work include *The Price Of Passion,* an erotic novella forthcoming from Firebrand, *AfterShocks,* a novel (Third Side Press), four volumes of short stories, and the parenting anthology, *Lesbians Raising Sons.*

ABOUT THE EDITORS

MICHELE KARLSBERG is a publicist and event planner for the lesbian, gay, and feminist literary community, and has been so for the past ten years. As the curator of the OUTSPOKEN: Gay and Lesbian Literary Series, she continues to help make visible both new and established writers. She feels that her best energy is put behind the voices that need to be heard. She divides her time between New York and San Francisco.

KAREN X. TULCHINSKY is the author of *Love Ruins Everything,* a novel (Press Gang), and *In Her Nature,* short fiction (The Women's Press), which was the 1996 winner of the VanCity Book Prize. She is the editor of *Friday The Rabbi Wore Lace: Jewish Lesbian Erotica* and *Hot & Bothered: Short Short Fiction On Lesbian Desire,* and co-editor of *Tangled Sheets* and *Queer View Mirror.* She teaches creative writing workshops and lives in Vancouver, Canada.